E. R. BRAITHWAITE

To Sir With Love

WITH AN INTRODUCTION BY
Caryl Phillips

D0230991

VINTAGE BOOKS
London

Published by Vintage 2005

20

Copyright © E. R. Braithwaite 1959
Introduction copyright © Caryl Phillips 2005

E. R. Braithwaite has asserted his right under the Copyright, Designs
and Patents Act, 1988 to be identified as the author of this work

First published in Great Britain in 1959 by The Bodley Head

Vintage
Random House, 20 Vauxhall Bridge Road,
London SW1V 2SA

www.vintage-classics.info

Addresses for companies within The Random House Group Limited
can be found at: www.randomhouse.co.uk/offices.htm

The Random House Group Limited Reg. No. 954009

A CIP catalogue record for this book
is available from the British Library

ISBN 9780099483694

Penguin Random House is committed to a sustainable future for
our business, our readers and our planet. This book is made from
Forest Stewardship Council® certified paper.

Printed and bound in Great Britain by Clays Ltd, Elcograf S.p.A.

TO SIR WITH LOVE

E. R. Braithwaite was born in 1912 in British Guiana and was educated there and in the United States. He served in the R.A.F during the Second World War and afterwards studied at the University of Cambridge where he received a Master's degree in Physics. His books include *To Sir With Love* (1959), *Paid Servant: A Report about Welfare Work in London* (1962), *A Kind of Home-Coming: A Visit to Africa* (1963), *A Choice of Straws* (1965), *Reluctant Neighbours* (1972), *Honorary White* (1975) and *Billingsly, The Bear with the Crinkled Ear* (2008). He represented Guiana at the United Nations in New York and later served as Ambassador to Venezuela. After he left the diplomatic service in 1970, he taught at various institutions in the United States including New York University, Florida State University and Howard University in Washington D. C., where he currently resides.

INTRODUCTION

TO SIR WITH LOVE (1959) was the first published book of Edward Ricardo Braithwaite, who was born in 1920 in British Guiana (present-day Guyana), the large English-speaking territory on the north-east coast of South America. His was a relatively comfortable upbringing, being the son of two Oxford-educated parents, and as a young man he quickly absorbed the conservative, middle-class manners of the Caribbean intellectual. He attended Queens College, an elite colonial school in British Guiana, and went on to study at City College in New York before enlisting as a Royal Air Force pilot in England. As Braithwaite states in *To Sir With Love*, like many other Caribbean men, he joined the British armed forces out of a sense of duty, and during the war years he was ready to die for *his* country.

Upon being demobilized at the end of the war, Braithwaite fully expects to be absorbed into the upper levels of his chosen profession of engineering. Not only has he studied in New York, but he will soon earn a Master's degree in Physics from Cambridge University. However, at interview after interview he is refused an appointment because of his colour. Unfortunately, the camaraderie of the service does not transfer to civilian life, and the realization of this fact strikes him a hard blow:

> I had just been brought face to face with something I had either forgotten or completely ignored for more than six exciting years – my black skin . . . Disappointment and

resentment were a solid bitter rising lump inside me; I hurried into the nearest public lavatory and was violently sick.

After eighteen months of unemployment and faltering confidence, Braithwaite decides to try teaching, for the profession is in desperate need of educated men and women. He successfully negotiates an interview, but then finds himself posted to one of the worst schools in the East End of London. He is further dismayed to discover that his charges are an unruly, disruptive group of fifteen-year-olds who stand cockily on the threshold of adulthood.

Braithwaite's somewhat haughty attitude to his new pupils is entirely predictable. After all, this is a man who, on the very first page of the book, has made it clear how superior he is, both intellectually and physically, to the disappointing English:

They reminded me somehow of the peasants in a book by Steinbeck: they were of the city, but they dressed like peasants, they looked like peasants, and they talked like peasants.

And, even before he has travelled out to the school, he muses aloud on the East End of London and wonders about its history in a manner that makes clear the extent of his distinguished education:

I had read references to it in both classical and contemporary writings and was eager to know the London of Chaucer and Erasmus and the Sorores Minores. I had dreamed of walking along the cobbled Street of the Cable Makers to the echoes of Chancellor and the brothers Willoughby. I wanted to look on the reach of the Thames at Blackwall from which Captain John Smith had sailed aboard the good ship *Susan Lawrence* to found an English colony in Virginia.

Predictably, the fetid air, and the dirty streets of the recently bombed-out East End disappoints, as do the unwashed, uncouth, youngsters now ranged before him. We are left in no doubt that Braithwaite's manners are impeccable, and that his dress is always smart and tidy, but it is also clear that an unmistakable, almost anthropological, sneer is permanently decorating the coloured teacher's face:

> The girl who rose to comply was fair-haired and slim, with a pair of heavy breasts which swung loosely under a thin jumper, evidently innocent of any support. I wondered at the kind of parent who would allow a girl to go out so sloppily attired.

There is, however, no doubt that Braithwaite would, during this period in the late forties and fifties, have had to endure a fair amount of anthropological sneering himself. *This* coloured man in London would be a double oddity; first for his colour, and then for his class. Those few West Indians who did occupy the streets of England would, despite the prejudice they endured, have had far more in common with white working-class people than with this Cambridge-educated former officer. In fact, throughout the course of the book there is no sense of 'Ricky' having a community of any sort beyond his white 'mum' and 'dad', and we do feel sympathy for this somewhat isolated, patrician, man who attempts now to make a community out of the pupils in his charge and his fellow teachers in the staffroom.

Braithwaite displays a great aptitude as a teacher, but we are aware that there are lessons the he too must learn, particularly with reference to humility and patience. Unsurprisingly, it is the *uncouth* pupils who begin to teach him. This is poignantly illustrated when the mother of one of the boys – the only mixed-race boy in the class – dies, and the pupils make it clear that although they are prepared to have a collection for a wreath, not one of them is able to deliver it, for to knock on the boy's door might be seen as fraternizing with coloureds. 'Ricky' is quick to fall into a trough of judgmental despair:

It was like a disease, and these children whom I loved without caring about *their* skins or *their* backgrounds, they were tainted with the hateful virus which attacked their vision, distorting everything that was not white or English.

I remembered a remark of Weston's: 'They're morons, cold as stone, nothing matters to them, nothing.'

I turned and walked out of the classroom sick at heart.

The following day, a still bitter Braithwaite turns up for the funeral:

And then I stopped, feeling suddenly washed clean, whole and alive again. Tears were in my eyes, unashamedly, for there, standing in a close, separate group on the pavement outside Seales' door was my class, my children, all or nearly all of them, smart and self-conscious in their best clothes. O God, forgive me for the hateful thoughts, because I love them, these brutal, disarming bastards, I love them . . .

Braithwaite also learns to be more tolerant of his fellow teachers, whose attitudes towards him vary from overt hostility to deep love. Navigating the choppy waters of the staffroom presents Braithwaite with almost as many problems as trying to control the pupils in the classroom, but eventually he succeeds in creating a place for himself in the school, and by the end of the book 'Sir' is both respected and loved by pupils and teachers alike.

However, beyond the confines of the school, British society is rife with serious problems of prejudice and bigotry, and it is to Braithwaite's credit that he points clearly to these issues. Although he manages to charm the local Yiddish-speaking shopkeeper, and win the heart of a fellow teacher and the grudging respect of her highly suspicious parents, he *is* shunned in the streets, he *is* often insulted by strangers, and he *is* made fully aware of the painful paradox of being 'British, but not being a Briton'. To Braithwaite's eyes, post-war British society is in trouble, and already he can see the profound difficulties that must be overcome before a truly multi-racial modern Britain can evolve, difficulties that, as it transpired, continued to plague the country for the whole of the second half of the twentieth century:

> They had been reared in a neighbourhood as multi-racial as anywhere in Britain, yet it had been of no significance to them. Some of them lived in the same street, the same block of flats, as Indians or Negroes, without ever even speaking to them, in obedience to the parental taboo. Others had known and grown up with coloured children through the Infant and Junior stages, but when the tensions and pretensions of puberty had intervened the relationship had ended.

Fifty years on, *To Sir With Love can* be read as a narrative of triumph over adversity concerning one highly unusual man's eight-month long experience of an inner-city school that enables him to grow, and occasions some of the people he comes into contact with to put their prejudices on hold. But clearly it is more than this. The author is keen for us to understand that the Ricky Braithwaites of this world can not, by themselves, uproot prejudice, but they can point to its existence. And this, after all, is the beginning of change; one must first identify the location of the problem before one can set about addressing it.

The author is also keen to remind us that in this post-war Britain, as in our own contemporary Britain, one wrong step and teacher 'Ricky' is just another nigger on the street. *To Sir With Love* leaves the reader in no doubt about the degree to which British society has, for centuries, been wedded to prejudice. Reading *To Sir With Love* reminds us that in the early fifties, as tens of thousands of easily identifiable 'others' were beginning to enter the country in an attempt to rebuild Britain after the ravages of the Second World War, this deep-seated problem of unquestioned hereditary prejudice was waiting to greet them in the streets, in the workplace, and in institutions of learning.

After the publication of *To Sir With Love*, E. R. Braithwaite left teaching and pursued a successful career as a social worker and then a diplomat. Reading this book it is easy to discern how well-suited he was to both careers. He also continued to produce books, including a memoir about his time as a social worker, *Paid Servant* (1962) and another about his time in South Africa, *Honorary White* (1975). However, partly because of the success of the filmed version of the book, *To Sir With Love* remains his best known work. This fine, and genuinely touching, portrait of a post-war English working-class community coming face to face with a decidedly atypical West Indian man, has much to tell us about race, class, and the education system in Britain. It also speaks eloquently to the individual courage of a Cambridge-educated West Indian who is prepared to share his own prejudices and fears as he trips cautiously across the rubble of the East End of London in those bleak, austere years following the end of the Second World War.

Caryl Phillips
New York City, May 2005

CHAPTER 1

THE CROWDED RED double-decker bus inched its way through the snarl of traffic in Aldgate. It was almost as if it was reluctant to get rid of the overload of noisy, earthy charwomen it had collected on its run through the city – thick-armed, bovine women, huge-breasted, with heavy bodies irrevocably distorted by frequent childbearing, faces pink and slightly damp from their early labours, the warm May morning and their own energy. There was a look of indestructibility about them, from the tip of each tinted head in its gaudy headscarf, tightly tied to expose one or two firmly fastened curls, to the solid legs and large feet which seemed rooted in the earth.

The women carried large heavy shopping bags, and in the ripe mixture of odours which accompanied them, the predominant one hinted at a good haul of fish or fishy things. They reminded me somehow of the peasants in a book by Steinbeck: they were of the city, but they dressed like peasants, they looked like peasants, and they talked like peasants. Their cows were motor-driven milk floats; their tools were mop and pail and kneeling pad; their farms a forest of steel and concrete. In spite of the hairgrips and headscarves, they had their own kind of dignity.

They joshed and chivvied each other and the conductor in an endless stream of lewdly suggestive remarks and retorts, quite careless of being overheard by me – a Negro, and the only other male on the bus. The conductor, a lively, quick-witted fellow, seemed to know them all well enough to

1

address them on very personal terms, and kept them in noisy good humour with a stream of quips and pleasantries to which they made reply in kind. Sex seemed little more than a joke to them, a conversation piece which alternated with their comments on the weather, and their vividly detailed discussions on their actual or imagined ailments.

I sat sandwiched between a window and a very large woman whose great dimpled arms hugged her shopping bag in her lap. She kept up a ribald duet with a crony sitting immediately in front of her.

'What've you got for the old Man's dinner, Gert?'

Gert's square body remained ponderously immobile, but she turned her head around as far as her massive neck would permit and rejoined:

'He'll be lucky to get bread and dripping today, he will.'

'He can't do you much good on bread and dripping, Gert.'

'Feeding him on steak and chicken won't make no difference neither, Rose. Never mind, he keeps me back warm.'

All this was said in a tone intentionally loud enough to entertain everyone, and the women showed their appreciation by cackling loudly, rocking their bodies as much as the crowding permitted. Rose turned her head to look fleetingly at me, then leaned forward to whisper rather audibly to Gert.

'Wouldn't mind having this lot in me stocking for Christmas, Gert.'

The chuckle which accompanied this remark shook every ounce of her like an ague, and I could feel it being conducted through the bus to me. Again Gert was forced to perform the trick of rotating her head against the uncompromisingly thick neck; her beady eyes slanted backward to bring me into orbit. She retorted, not so loudly.

'Aw, give over Rose, you wouldn't know what to do with it, you've been a widow too long.'

'Speak for yourself, Gert,' Rose replied gaily. ''S like riding a bicycle, you never forget how. You wouldn't credit it, but I figure I could teach him a thing or two.'

'Hark at her,' Gert enjoined the bus at large, who were

sharing delightedly in this byplay. 'Never mind, Rose, I'll send me Alfie round to see you one of these nights; he's not too bad when he gets round to it.'

Unable to resist the amusement I felt, I smiled inwardly at the essential naturalness of these folk who were an integral part of one of the world's greatest cities and at the same time as common as hayseeds. There they sat, large and vigorous, the bulwark of the adventurous.

The smile must have shown on my face, for Rose glanced at me in some surprise, then leaned forward to whisper in Gert's ear. She in turn whispered to her neighbour and soon there was a chain reaction of whispers and giggles and nudgings, as if they were somewhat surprised to discover that I had understood every word. I felt sure they could not care one way or the other; these people who had lived too intimately with poverty and danger and death would not be easily embarrassed.

The bus swung around Gardiner's Corner and along Commercial Road. Its pace was quicker now, and the chit-chat began to flag as other thoughts intervened. At each stop now they were disembarking, returning to their homes in the strange, rather forbidding deep tangle of narrow streets and alleyways which led off from the main thoroughfare in a disordered unpremeditated pattern. Through the window I watched the fleeting panorama of dingy shopfronts and cafés with brave large superscriptions telling of faraway places. The long Commercial Road lay straight ahead, fluttering like an international maypole with the name ribbons of Greece and Israel, Poland and China, Germany and Belgium, India and Russia, and many others; Semmelweiss and Smaile, Schultz and Chin-Yen, Smith, Seibt and Litobaraki.

The bus eased to a stop. Rose shifted her shopping bag off her lap and with a grunt levered her ponderous body upright; she smiled broadly at me, and with a cheery 'Ta Gert, ta girls', she waddled towards the exit while I eased my shoulders in relief from the confining pressure of her body. God, what a huge woman.

As the bus moved slowly on, a bright-eyed little boy in

school cap and blazer paused momentarily beside the vacant seat and then quickly moved a little way on in courteous deference to a slim, smartly dressed woman who followed behind. As I looked up she smiled her thanks to him and was preparing to sit when her eyes met mine. Surprise flickered briefly on her face as she straightened up and moved forward to stand in the narrow aisle beside the boy, who looked up at her with a puzzled expression.

The conductor approached with his cheery 'Any more fares, please, free ride only after midnight.' He had been keeping the charwomen entertained by such witticisms throughout the journey. The woman reached into her bag, and the conductor casually remarked as he took her fare:

'Empty seat beside you, lady.'

She received her ticket with a murmured 'Thank you,' but gave no sign that she had heard him.

'Seat here for you, lady.'

The conductor indicated the vacant place with a turn of his head and moved on to examine the boy's school pass and exchange a word with the youngster. On his way back he paused to look at the woman, who returned his gaze with the cool effrontery of a patrician.

'No standing on the bus, lady.'

The conductor's voice was deliberately louder, with an angry rasp to it; the charladies twisted and craned their necks in their efforts to discover the reason for his sudden brusqueness. The slim woman remained standing, cool, remote, undismayed by the conductor's threatening attitude or the pointedly hostile glances directed at her by the women in their immediate sympathy and solidarity with the conductor against someone who was obviously not of their class. My quick anger at the woman's undisguised prejudice was surprisingly tinctured by a certain admiration for her fearless, superior attitude; she was more than a match for them. What a superior bitch! She looked the conductor straight in the eye and around her mouth I could discern the muscular twitchings of a suppressed smile. I guessed she was secretly enjoying herself. What a smooth, elegant, superior bitch!

Just ahead I saw a nameplate on a building, New Road. I quickly rose and said to the conductor, 'Next stop, please.' He gave me an odd disapproving stare, as if I had in some way betrayed him by leaving before he could have a real set-to with the woman; I sensed that he would have liked to try humiliating her, even to putting her off the bus. He pulled the bell-cord and the bus jerked to a stop, and as I stepped off the platform I saw the woman take the seat I had just vacated, stiff backed and unruffled. By leaving I had done that conductor a favour, I thought. He'd never get the better of that female.

The bus pulled away from the stop, but I remained standing there, feeling suddenly depressed by the prospect around me. I suppose I had entertained some naïvely romantic ideas about London's East End, with its cosmopolitan population and fascinating history. I had read references to it in both classical and contemporary writings and was eager to know the London of Chaucer and Erasmus and the Sorores Minores. I had dreamed of walking along the cobbled Street of the Cable Makers to the echoes of Chancellor and the brothers Willoughby. I wanted to look on the reach of the Thames at Blackwall from which Captain John Smith had sailed aboard the good ship *Susan Lawrence* to found an English colony in Virginia. I had dreamed. . . .

But this was different. There was nothing romantic about the noisy littered street bordered by an untidy irregular picket fence of slipshod shopfronts and gaping bomb sites. I crossed Commercial Road at the traffic lights into New Road. This was even worse. The few remaining buildings, raped and outraged, were still partly occupied, the missing glass panes replaced by clapboard or brightly coloured squares of tinplate advertising Brylcreem, Nugget Shoe Polish and Palm Toffee. There was rubble everywhere, and dirt and flies. And there were smells.

The smells arose from everything, everywhere, flowing together and remaining as a sickening, tantalizing discomfort. They flowed from the delicatessen shop with its uncovered trays of pickled herrings, and the small open casks of pickled gherkins and onions, dried fish and salted meat, and sweaty damp walls and floor; from the fish shop which casually defied every law of health; from the Kosher butcher, and the poulterer next door where a fine confetti of new plucked feathers hung nearly motionless in the fetid air; and from sidewalk gutters where multitudes of flies buzzed and feasted on the heaped-up residue of fruit and vegetable barrows.

I felt sick and dirtied; only the need of reaching my destination forced me along past the shops and the smells and the multi-racial jostle of hurrying folk who ignored the flies and smells in single-minded pursuit of their business.

Near the railway viaduct the line of buildings on both sides of New Road came to an abrupt halt; the bustling thoroughfare now bisected a desert of rubble and rubbish which Nature had hurriedly and inadequately tried to camouflage with quick-sprouting weeds, shrubs and ragged grass. Here and there could be seen the rusty skeleton of a spring mattress or a child's pram, a cracked toilet bowl and a dented steel helmet, American style – relics of peace and war humbled together in rust and decay. The flies were here, too, and so were several small children, too young for school, but old and venturesome enough to grub in this perilous playground. Their eyes shone happily in grimy faces as they laughed, screamed and fought in rivalry with each other.

The games overflowed on to the sidewalk and I walked wide around a 'ring-a-ring-o'-roses' who smiled happily up at me without interrupting their noisy chant. They could not have known that from their happy faces, dirty but unafraid, I took courage for the new experience I was about to face.

I soon located the narrow alleyway with the legend:

'Greenslade Secondary School,
A. Florian. Headmaster.'

This alleyway opened on to a small macadam forecourt, along one side of which was a green outhouse labelled 'BOYS'. From it emerged a small, dark-haired, elfin-faced boy. He was dressed in blue jeans and a discoloured once-white T-shirt, and on seeing me he attempted to hide the cigarette stub which he held pinched between forefinger and thumb of his right hand.

'Looking for somebody?' His Cockney voice was high-pitched and comic.

'Looking for somebody, mate?' he said again. The right hand was now safely in the pocket of the jeans, though a tell-tale wisp of blue smoke tendrilled its way up the skinny forearm.

'Where can I find Mr Florian, the Headmaster?'

I could hardly keep the amusement out of my voice at the ill-concealed cigarette.

'Straight up those stairs,' and with a casual gesture the boy pointed, cigarette stub and all, towards a half-closed doorway across the forecourt. I thanked him and moved towards the door.

The stairway ended outside a green door on which was a small white card bearing the information:

'Alex Florian. Headmaster. Please knock and come in.'

I knocked and hesitated; a somewhat impatient voice said, 'Come in, it's open.'

Behind a large desk sat a small man whose large head was decorated with a fine crop of carefully groomed curly white hair; the face was either tanned or olive-skinned, lean with high cheekbones and surprisingly smooth, as if the youth-fulness which had deserted his hair had found permanent accommodation around the aquiline nose and full sensuous mouth; his brown eyes were large, slightly protruding, and seemed filled with a kind of wonder, as if he were on the verge of some new and exciting discovery.

I approached his desk and he stood to greet me, but that produced very little difference in his stature and I noticed that he was short and somewhat hunchbacked. He was carefully, even nattily dressed, and there was about him and the room a very pleasant orderliness quite at variance with the external surroundings. He extended a pale, strong-fingered hand and remarked smiling, 'You're Braithwaite, I suppose, we've been expecting you. Do sit down.' I was later to learn that the remark was typical of the man; he considered himself merely one of a team engaged in important and necessary work; he was spokesman and official representative of the team, but sought no personal aggrandisement because of that. I shook hands with him and settled down in the chair, pleased and reassured by the sincere warmth of his greeting. He opened a box on his desk and offered me a cigarette; when we had both lit up he leaned back in his seat and began:

'Hope you found this place without much difficulty; we're rather hidden away in this little backwoods and many people have had a hard time locating us.'

'I have had no difficulty, thank you. I followed the rather detailed directions I got at the Divisional Office.'

'Good. Anyway, we're glad to have you. I hope that when you've had a chance to look at us you'll be just as pleased to stay.'

'Not much doubt about that, Sir,' I hastened to assure him.

He smiled at my eagerness and said:

'Anyhow, I think it would be best if you had a good look around the school first, and then we'll talk about it. Things are done here somewhat differently from the usual run, and many teachers have found it, shall we say, disquieting. Wander around just as you please, and see what's going on, and if you then decide to remain with us, we'll talk about it after lunch.'

With that he got up and led me to the door, his eyes dancing like those of a mischievous imp; I stepped out and he closed it behind me.

CHAPTER 2

FROM THE HEADMASTER'S office a short flight of stairs led down to a narrow corridor between the Auditorium on one side and some classrooms on the other. I paused for a moment outside the first of these classrooms, not sure where to begin, when the door was pushed violently outwards and a tall, red-headed girl rushed out into the corridor closely pursued by two others. In such a narrow space I was quite unable to dodge her wild progress, so I quickly grabbed her by the arms both to avoid being bowled over and to steady her. Quickly recovering herself she shook loose, smiled impudently in my face, and with a quick 'Sorry' raced down the corridor and out of sight. Her companions pulled up hastily, stopped a moment to look at me, then quickly re-entered the classroom, letting the door bang loudly shut behind them.

I was staggered by this unexpected encounter and remained where I was for a moment, unsure of what to do next. Then, deciding to take a closer look at what went on in that room, I knocked on the door, opened it and walked in. There was a general hubbub and for a little while no one seemed aware of my entry, and then, very gradually, one by one the occupants turned to stare at me.

There was no sign of anyone who looked like a teacher. About forty boys and girls were in the room. Perhaps it would be more accurate to call them young men and women, for there was about most of them a degree of adulthood, not only in terms of obvious physical development, but also in the way their clothes were worn to emphasise that development wherever possible. They stood around the room in casual postures; some were clustered around a large open empty fireplace in one corner; a few were sitting on desks or chairs in careless unscholarly attitudes. They nearly all wore a kind of unofficial uniform. Among the girls, proud of bust and uplift brassière, this took the form of too-tight sweaters and too-long clinging skirts and flat-heeled shoes. A wide variety of hairstyles paid tribute to their particular screen favourite. It was all a bit soiled and untidy, as if too little attention were paid to washing either themselves or their flashy finery. The boys wore blue jeans and T-shirts or open-necked plaid shirts.

A large, round-faced, freckled girl left the group by the fireplace and approached me.

'If you're looking for Mr Hackman, he's not here, he's in the staffroom,' she announced. 'He said when we are ready to behave one of us can go and call him.'

The various groups began to disintegrate and reform on either side of this self-elected spokesman, and I was subjected to their bold, unabashed scrutiny. God, I thought, what a crowd! Suddenly they were talking all at once, as if a penny had finally dropped somewhere; the questions came thick and fast.

'Are you the new teacher?'

'Are you taking Old Hack's place?'

'Is old Hackman really leaving?'

Taking my cue from the fat girl's first remark I said: 'I think I'll look in at the staffroom,' and slipped quickly through the door. I felt shocked by the encounter. My vision of teaching in a school was one of straight rows of desks, and neat, well-mannered, obedient children. The room I had just left seemed like a menagerie. What kind of fellow could this Hackman be who would stand for that sort of behaviour? Was it the accepted thing here? Would I have to accept it too?

With these disturbing thoughts I walked down the corridor towards some double doors which I guessed would lead in the general direction of the staffroom; as I approached them they were opened by the red-head, who swished imperiously past on her way back to her classroom. I turned to look at the retreating figure topped by long auburn hair caught up in a pony-tail which jerked in time to her vigorous, hip-swaying stride. Mr Florian's cryptic remarks were beginning to make a lot of sense; things were certainly different around here.

The staffroom lay up a short flight of stairs beyond the end of the corridor; the door was open. Reclining in an easy chair, fingers interlocked behind his head, was a large, hairy, cadaverous, young man, in baggy grey flannel slacks and a well-worn hacking jacket with leather patches at the elbows and wrists. A maroon shirt and yellow large-knotted tie did nothing to dispel the air of general untidiness which enveloped him. As I entered he looked up at me and remarked:

'Ah, another lamb to the slaughter – or shall we say black sheep?'

In appreciation of his own witticism he smiled broadly, exposing some large, uneven, yellow teeth.

I have always been subject to quick explosive anger, but for years I have been making a determined attempt to exercise close control of my temper. So now I watched this fellow, ready, willing and, I hope, able to take a joke about myself.

'My name's Braithwaite. I'm from the Divisional Office.'

'So you're the new teacher,' he replied. 'Hope you have better luck with the bastards than Hackman did.'

'I thought you were Hackman, because some of the children said he was waiting here until one of them called him.'

'He was, for about ten seconds, then he girded up his loins and departed.' He grinned. 'I expect that by now he is pouring out his woes to the Divisional Officer.'

'What happens to his class now?' I enquired.

At this he guffawed loudly. 'Without being too prophetic, I'd say you're for it.'

While I digested this little bit of frightening information he got up and left the room.

For some time after his departure I stood there watching the door; this was all very different from anything I had expected

11

and far from reassuring. But I had no intention of being scared away so easily. This fellow with his air of studied carelessness and his chatter was evidently a poseur; perhaps he'd improve on acquaintance. No harm in hoping.

The door opened to admit a tall blonde woman, dressed in a close-fitting white overall which somehow succeeded in flattering her already attractive figure. Her face was saved from plainness by large clear grey eyes and shapely mouth which denied the severity of the tight bun at the nape of her neck. She smiled and moved towards me with outstretched hand.

'Oh, hello! I suppose you're the new teacher from Divisional Office?'

'Yes, my name's Braithwaite.'

'Mine's Dale-Evans, Mrs Grace Dale-Evans. The hyphen is very important, especially when I use it to impress my grocer in the middle of the month.' Her voice was low-pitched and pleasant. 'Have you seen the Old Man?'

'Mr Florian? Yes, I've seen him; he suggested I take a look around to sort of see what's going on.'

'Have you seen any of the children yet?'

'Just a quick look. I popped into Mr Hackman's classroom on my way up here.'

'Oh, did you? A bit rough, don't you think? I take them for Domestic Science, not very scientific but domestic enough for them.'

While talking she was busily collecting cups from the mantelpiece, floor and windowsill and placing them in the small sink which occupied one corner of the room. An Ascot heated supplied hot water over the sink, and soon she was washing up and talking over the clatter of crockery.

'Some teachers are as bad as the kids; leave their cups wherever they sit. Oh, sorry, please take a seat.'

I sat and watched her deft movements with the tiny dishmop and later the dishcloth.

'Been teaching long?'

'Not really. Actually this is my first appointment.'

'Ouch.' She grimaced. 'Don't go too highbrow on me; we

12

call them jobs, not appointments,' and she laughed, a pleasant lazy sound, unexpectedly at variance with the staccato crispness of her speech.

'Ex-service?'

'Yes, R.A.F. aircrew. Why?'

'Oh, just something about you. Staying to dinner?'

'I hadn't thought of it, but if it's usual I'd like to.'

'Good, I'll pop across and have a word with the school secretary. She'll be able to fix it, I'm sure. Stay here if you like and meet the others at recess. Nearly time now. See you then.' She went out and closed the door quietly behind her.

I looked around the room. It was small and untidy with piles of books everywhere. One wall was occupied by a large open cupboard, cluttered up with a miscellany of sports goods – footballs, netballs, and table tennis gear, plimsolls, boxing gloves and string-tied bundles of soiled denim P.T. trunks. In and around the cold fireplace was a litter of cigarette butts with and without lipstick. Coats, umbrellas and satchels festooned one wall. Seven or eight easy chairs, two straight-backed wooden chairs and a large centrally placed table completed the furniture. It was stuffy from stale cigarette smoke and a mixture of body smells, so I walked over and opened the two sash windows which overlooked the gutted remains of a bomb-wrecked church, squatting among a mixture of weed-choked gravestones and rubble. A rusty iron fence separated this peaceful chaos from a small well-ordered park, trim with neat flower beds, and restful with a variety of large trees now in heavy foliage; but that this little park had also once been part of the churchyard was proved by the rows of headstones arranged with military precision along one wall of the park, overlooking the tiny lawns and flower beds beneath which long-forgotten bones still lay in peace. A high brick wall separated the school from the churchyard.

I left the staffroom and followed the stairs down to the ground floor and passed through a doorway out into the macadam courtyard. It was littered with crumpled paper bags, apple cores, sweet wrappers and bits of newspaper; great blobs of mucus everywhere indicated that nearly every child was probably suffering from a heavy cold. This courtyard-cum-playground ran along three sides of the school and was about twenty or twenty-five feet wide. The high wall surrounding it met the churchyard wall at right angles and separated the school premises from a rag-merchant's yard and a firm of contractors on either side, and also from the untidy backyards of a long row of dilapidated lodging houses which, except for two narrow alleyways, completely sealed off the front of the school from the busy street. Although it was a bright, sunny morning, the courtyard was partly in deep shadow, and the atmosphere of the whole place was depressing, like a prison. The school rose out of the courtyard, a solid, unpretentious, rather dirty structure, no taller than its neighbours. Its two entrance doors, one opposite each alleyway, were painted a dark, unfriendly green, as were the boys' and girls' lavatories which squatted in separate corners of the courtyard, as if aware that, like the large, ash-filled dustbins, they were usurping precious playing space.

My depression deepened and I thought how very different all this was from my own childhood schooldays spent in warm, sunny Georgetown. There, in a large rambling wooden school-house, light and cool within, surrounded by wide, tree-shaded lawns on which I had romped with my fellows in vigorous contentment, I spent rich, happy days, filled with the excitement of learning, each new little achievement a personal adventure and a source of satisfaction to my interested parents. How did these East London children feel about coming to this forbidding-looking place, day after day? Were they as eagerly excited about school as I had been when a boy?

The sound of a handbell interrupted my thoughts, and shortly afterwards there were the sounds of banging doors, hurrying feet, clattering of milk bottles, talk and laughter as the children erupted out of their classrooms for the morning recess. I hurried inside and up towards the staffroom, but halfway up the gloomy stairway I was forced to stand against one wall by the crush of children which spilled down the stairs towards the playground in a noisy, jostling tangle, pushing me aside with no more consideration than was shown to their fellows.

When I reached the staffroom Mrs Dale-Evans was preparing tea. She looked up at my entry and remarked:

'Oh, hello! Tea will be ready in a moment; the rest of the staff will soon drift in and then I'll introduce you.'

I walked over to a window and stood looking across at the ruined church and the innumerable pigeons which strutted in and out of its damaged cupola.

One by one the teachers turned up and were soon seated about the room, sipping their tea and exchanging chit-chat on the morning's activities. On seeing me they murmured the usual sounds of greeting, and when they were all there I was introduced to each one in turn. As we moved from one to another Mrs Dale-Evans both surprised and embarrassed me by commenting on each individual in a barely audible aside.

Miss Josy Dawes, short for Josephine, was the first to be introduced. She was a shortish strong-looking young woman, whose plain square face was unrelieved by make-up and fringed by dark hair cut very short, which added to her rather mannish appearance. She wore an open-necked short-sleeved man's shirt, against which her prominent breasts clamoured for attention, a severe skirt in heavy grey flannel, ankle-length socks and sturdy low-heeled brown brogue shoes. Her voice in greeting was deep, resonant and quite pleasing.

Next came Miss Euphemia Phillips, youngish and mousy. There was something of an immature school-girl about her round face, in which her large grey eyes held a mixture of helplessness and expectancy. Her rather gay woollen dress emphasised the immaturity of her slight figure.

'Good Lord,' I thought, 'how does this one cope in a school like this?' Those girls I saw earlier on were much taller and outweighed her by a wide margin.

As we approached Theo Weston, he smiled in what was meant to be a friendly manner, though it was hard to discern it behind the thicket of ginger-coloured beard.

'Fancy being able to shave off your manhood whenever you like,' murmured Mrs Dale-Evans in my ear.

'I had the pleasure of welcoming Mr Braithwaite to our *ménage*,' said Weston. His voice was surprisingly thin and squeaky. 'He mistook me for Hackman.'

'By the way,' someone asked, 'where *is* the dear boy?'

'Escaped,' Weston replied. 'Fled, quit. I don't think he even tarried long enough to bid the Old Man a fond farewell.'

'When did all this happen?'

'I had a free period this morning,' Weston continued, 'and soon after ten Hackman barged in here looking like all the Furies, collected his coat and the newspaper I was reading, and departed. I'll wager we never see that colleague again.'

'Oh, well,' Mrs Dale-Evans shrugged, 'they come and they go. Let's meet the others.'

She took me by the arm and led me up to Mrs Drew, a white-haired matron, elegant from the tip of her softly permed head to her neat well-shod feet. She looked capable and as solid as Gibraltar.

'One of the best. She's the Old Man's deputy,' whispered Mrs Dale-Evans.

We passed on to Miss Vivienne Clintridge, art and drama teacher, a chubby, well-formed thirtyish brunette who exuded a certain brash animal charm. As we shook hands I was amazed to see myself reflected in her large smiling brown eyes. Her voice in greeting was silvery with acceptance and immediate friendliness.

'Clinty's an excellent artist, but teaching has to provide the bread and butter.' I wondered if anyone had overheard these comments from Mrs Dale-Evans.

The last to be introduced was Miss Gillian Blanchard. Every man has his own idea of beauty. Many years ago I visited the Caribbean island of Martinique and there saw what I still believe to be the world's most beautiful women; tall, willowy, graceful creatures with soft wavy raven hair and skin the colour of honey. Gillian Blanchard was lovely in the same kind of way: tall, her hair cut in a black neat skull-cap, full-figured, elegant. Her skin had a rich olive tint which hinted at Jewish or Italian parentage. Dark eyes, nearly black in the depths of them. Lovely.

'She's new here,' Mrs Dale-Evans whispered, 'came last Wednesday.'

When I had met them all I moved over to the window nearest the sink and stood listening to the rise and fall of talk, which was mainly concerned with classroom goings-on. Miss Clintridge leaned against the fireplace and held forth in a rather loud voice on the artistic endeavours of her morning class, with here and there an amusingly Freudian interpretation. Miss Dawes and Miss Phillips sat in a corner, somewhat removed from the group around the fireplace, in earnest whispered conversation with each other. Presently Mrs Drew came over to me, a cigarette held daintily in her long, manicured fingers.

'I hope you're going to stay with us, Mr Braithwaite.'

I looked at her kindly, earnest face and smiled without replying.

'We've had a succession of men teachers here in the past year, none staying longer than a term or two,' she continued. 'It's been hard on the boys, the bigger ones especially; they do need the firmer handling of men.' At this point Miss Clintridge left the group by the fireplace and came over to us.

'Did I hear someone say "Men"?' she enquired, grinning as she perched her behind on the edge of the sink.

'I was telling Mr Braithwaite how really hard up we are for some good men teachers. Now that Mr Hackman's left things would be rather difficult without a replacement.'

Miss Clintridge snorted. 'I wouldn't use the words good men teachers and Hackman in the same breath. Anyway, talking of being hard up, you speak for yourself, ducks! I'll tell him my own hard luck story, if he's interested.' Her laughter was sweet, friendly and guileless.

'Do be serious, Clinty.' Mrs Drew was smiling in spite of herself. 'The idea is to encourage him to stay, not frighten him away.'

'Gosh, why didn't you tell me? I could be very encouraging if I tried,' and she suited action to words with puckered lips and arched eyebrows. The laughter bubbled out of me at these antics, in spite of my intentions to maintain my reserve.

'You will stay, won't you?' Miss Clintridge continued in more serious vein.

'I think I'd like to,' I replied rather lamely, secretly amused at these enquiries, because actually I was so pleased to land this appointment that the likelihood of refusing it would hardly have occurred to me. But these people evidently expected some hesitation on my part, and I considered it more prudent to humour them.

'Good.' She jumped down from her perch on the sink as the bell sounded the end of recess. 'Now the bigger girls will have something else to think about for a while; that should keep them out of our hair.' She winked at Mrs Drew and rushed off to her duties, as did all the others except Miss Blanchard, who was busy marking books from a pile on the floor beside her chair.

After the noisy chatter of a few moments ago the room was so quiet that the scratch of her pen and the rustle of turned pages sounded quite loud. After a while she turned and looked up at me.

'Won't you sit down?'

I moved over and sat in the chair beside her.

'This your first appointment?' Her voice was low, well-modulated, a brown voice. She'd said 'appointment'. As she spoke she closed the notebook she had marked, set it on the pile beside her, and leaned back in her chair with her hands lightly folded in her lap. Quiet, controlled hands.

'Yes. But why is everyone so doubtful and concerned about my remaining here?'

'I couldn't answer that, I'm afraid. You see, I've only been here a short time myself – three days, to be exact.' Definitely a brown voice; molasses, corn-pone, sapodilla brown. A nice voice.

'They said the same thing to me,' she continued. 'And now I'm beginning to understand why. There's something rather odd about this school, something rather frightening and challenging at the same time.' I had the feeling that she was speaking more to herself than to me.

'There's no corporal punishment here, or any other form of

punishment for that matter, and the children are encouraged to speak up for themselves. Unfortunately, they're not always particularly choosy about the things they say, and it can be rather alarming and embarrassing. Not every teacher's cup of tea, I imagine, though Miss Clintridge and Mrs Dale-Evans seem not to mind that sort of thing; I think they're themselves both East Londoners, and are not too easily shocked.'

'Are the children difficult to manage?'

Even as I asked it I realised how trite the question was, but I wanted her to go on talking, less for the information I might acquire than for the sheer pleasure of listening to her.

'I find them difficult, but then, you see, I've no real experience of teaching. They're so frightfully grown-up and sure of themselves, I think I'm a little bit afraid of them. The boys are not bad, but the girls have a way of looking at me, sort of pityingly, as if they're so much older and wiser than I am. I think they're more interested in my clothes and private life than anything I try to teach them.' Her voice quavered and she closed her eyes; the long lashes were a fringed pattern against her tanned skin.

The door opened to admit Mrs Dale-Evans, who smiled at us and began bustling about in what was evidently her familiar routine of collecting cups and washing them.

'Got to fix a bath presently, for the Murphy girl in Clinty's class. Kids complaining again, won't sit near her. Some mothers ought to be shot. Child stinks. A pity.'

I felt that she expected some comment from one of us.

'What's the matter with the child?' I asked. 'Enuretic?'

'God, no. Been wearing the same sanitary napkin for days, I guess. Fourteen years old and as helpless as an infant. You men teachers don't know how lucky you are; the things we women have to do for these kids.' And she lifted her eyes in mute supplication to Heaven.

The washing done, she came over to us, wiping her hands with a towel. 'Show you around my domain if you like.'

I stood up, excused myself from Miss Blanchard, and followed Mrs Dale-Evans out of the staffroom.

The Domestic Science Department was a large well-equipped room on the top floor and evidently her pride and joy; she showed off the gleaming gas cookers, pots and pans, the rows of well scrubbed heavy deal tables, the pedal sewing machines and the washing machines all spick and span in their places like guardsmen paraded for inspection. Along one wall were rows of drawers containing cutlery and all the paraphernalia of the housewife's art. From the roof, at intervals, hung about a dozen rubber-sheathed electric cables each of which ended in a protected socket ready to receive an electric iron. In a tiny alcove sectioned off from the rest of the room was a child's cot in which lay a life-size baby-doll, and on a table nearby were neatly laid out the general equipment for the care of the baby. She kept up a running commentary on everything I saw, and at this point remarked, waving her hand at the cot in the alcove: 'Some of them know more about this lot than I do; regular bunch of little mothers they are; call this "fancy stuff".'

As we were speaking a group of girls arrived for their cookery lesson. They were ordered to scrub their hands thoroughly at the sink, after which they stood quietly behind the deal tables while Mrs Dale-Evans explained the simple recipe she wished them to follow.

I remained with her, marvelling at the high standard of cleanliness and order she was able to achieve with the children. If she could accomplish such near perfection without recourse to beatings, then I would most certainly have a shot at it. This woman with her ready, listening ear and proven, sound advice, was both teacher and mother to these girls. But I felt certain that, should the occasion arise, she could also be tough – very tough.

CHAPTER 3

THE DINING HALL-cum-gymnasium extended over most of the ground floor. We entered and sat at a table slightly apart from the rows of folding tables occupied by the children. When everyone was assembled, Mr Florian stood up and said grace: 'For what we are about to receive may the Lord make us truly thankful.' The chorused 'Amen' which followed was lost in the din of rattling cutlery, chatter of children, and clanging of pots and pans as the kitchen staff filled and refilled the tureens.

The children were seated in groups of eight, two of them in turn being responsible for collecting and distributing the food for their particular group. Both boys and girls took turns at this and showed remarkable skill in portioning each course evenly and quickly. At the end of each course the day's two servers stacked the dishes, collected the cutlery and rushed them away to the kitchen staff. At the end of the meal the tablecloths were shaken and folded, and each group sat quietly awaiting the signal of dismissal.

When we were all finished Mr Florian rose and there was an immediate hush; at a signal from him the children stood and group by group left the dining hall quietly. I followed the others up to the staffroom, where Mrs Dale-Evans was soon busy preparing a cup of tea.

I stood at a window looking across to the ruined church, until a loud blare of swing music from close at hand caused me to turn round. Noticing the look of enquiry on my face, Miss Clintridge said:

21

'That's the midday dance session. The kids are allowed to use the hall from one to one forty-five each day; they play the records on a gramophone pick-up through the wireless loudspeaker. Sometimes I join them, and so does Grace. Even the Old Man shakes a leg on occasions.'

'That, my dear newcomer, is the understatement of the year.' Weston's voice was as shrill as his person was untidy. 'It is grossly unfair of you, Clinty, to mislead our sunburned friend with so innocent a remark. One look at those energetic morons should convince him that they're not dancing for the fun of it.' He slowly pulled himself out of his chair and leaned indolently against the fireplace. Everyone was now watching him. 'They're ever so cute. Dancing is the voluntary exercise by which they keep themselves fit for the more exciting pastime of teacher-baiting. The music seems somewhat louder than usual, so one can suppose they're having a sort of celebration jamboree over the abdication of our late but not lamented colleague.'

'What a ham you are, Weston,' Miss Clintridge remarked.

'Take no notice of Mr Weston,' Mrs Drew's voice was even and controlled. 'He will have his little joke.'

Weston smiled sweetly. 'Well,' he said: 'One way or another our fine feathered friend will soon learn for himself. Let us hope that he fares better than some of his predecessors.'

'Don't you think you might be a little less discouraging, Weston?' Mrs Dale-Evans cut in.

Weston raised both his arms heavenwards in mock solemnity. 'You do me an injustice, Grace dear,' he bleated pleasantly. 'The last thing I want to do is discourage him. After all, none of us would want to be saddled with that crowd of, shall we say, blithe spirits, would we?'

'I wonder if they'll advertise Hackman's job,' interrupted Mrs Drew. Her remark set them chattering all at once, and I moved towards the door, remembering that the Headmaster expected me in his office. Miss Blanchard reached it ahead of me, and together we went out into a barrage of sound.

'Odd fish, don't you think?' Even though raised above the intruding blare of trumpet, her voice was pleasing, and warm.

'Do you mean Weston?'

'Him, and others. I strongly suspect I would have slapped his face if he had dared to speak to me like that.' She spoke with a quiet confidence which left no doubt that she would have done just that. 'He hasn't scared you off, I hope?'

I turned to look at her, but could read nothing in her frank, impersonal glance. All the same, I felt a bit irritated by that remark.

We moved a little way into the auditorium and the rush of sound hit me like a blow. Four couples and about twenty pairs of girls were jiving to the music of an inspired trumpet player. Faces taut and expressionless, mouths slightly agape, skirts cartwheeled out, they spinned and reversed in the spontaneous intricacies of the dance, with an easy confident dove-tailing of movement which suggested long and frequent practice. Several boys were seated on low forms set alongside one wall, watching the dancers and whispering among themselves, pointing with their eyes at the generous leg exposure which their worm's eye view afforded. The dancers, I thought, were well aware of this, and strove to outdo each other for this attention.

Against the insinuating pulsation of the drums the muted trumpet urged the dancers on: even the low-level watchers kept up the tempo with a soft, rhythmic clapping, or a quick twitching of haunches and shoulders. I felt a desire to join them growing on me.

'They're good, aren't they?' Miss Blanchard's whisper was close to my ear. 'I wish I could dance as well as that.'

I turned to her. 'Would you like to try?'

'What, me, here?'

There was both surprise and a certain disgust in her tone, and I turned again to watch the dancers, as they disengaged themselves to move into little groups, chatting and laughing while awaiting a change of record. One of them moved away from a group and approached us; it was the red-headed girl with whom I had collided earlier that morning. There was something uncomfortably compelling about her full figure, clear skin, and casual wide-legged stance as she stopped in front of me and enquired: 'Can you jive?'

I was quite unprepared for this, and quickly muttered something in what I hope was polite refusal. The girl looked coolly into my face, then pirouetted lightly on her heel and sashayed back to rejoin her friends, her clear laugh floating back in her wake with the opening bars of the next record.

I turned to Miss Blanchard, but she must have slipped away when the girl approached me, so I quickly steered my way through the dancers, disturbed and excited at the prospect and challenge of having to cope with such nearly adult individuals.

Mr Florian was sitting at his desk juggling with a small object. When I was seated, he extended it for my inspection – an ugly little nude statuette in green mottled earthenware. 'Terrible, isn't it? Picked it up in Austria some time ago; been trying to break the damned thing for ages.' With a sigh he set it down with exaggerated care on his desk.

'Well, what is it to be?' His glance was kindly but direct.

'I'll have a shot at it,' I replied, carefully moderating my enthusiasm.

'Good, now let's get you into the picture.' And with a crisp economy of words he outlined his policy for the school.

'You may have heard some talk about this school, Braithwaite. We're always being talked about, but unfortunately most of the talk is by ill-informed people who are intolerant of the things we are trying to do.

'The majority of the children here could be generally classified as difficult, probably because in junior schools they have shown some disregard for, or opposition to, authority. Whether or not that authority was well-constituted is beside the point; it is enough to say that it depended largely on fear, either of the stick or some other form of punishment. In the case of these children it failed. We in this school believe that children are merely men and women in process of development; and that that development, in all its aspects, should be neither forced nor restricted at the arbitrary whim of any individual who by some accident of fortune is in a position to exercise some authority over them.

'The children in this area have always been poorly fed,

clothed and housed. By the very nature of their environment they are subject to many pressures and tensions which tend to inhibit their spiritual, moral and physical growth, and it is our hope and intention to try to understand something of those pressures and tensions, and in understanding, to help them.

'First of all we must appreciate that the total income of many of these families is quite insufficient to provide for them the minimum of food, warmth and dry shelter necessary for good health. Some of these children are from homes where the so-called breadwinner is chronically unemployed, or, in some cases, quite uninterested in seeking employment. As a result, meals are irregular and of very poor quality. A child who has slept all night in a stuffy, overcrowded room, and then breakfasts on a cup of weak tea and a piece of bread, can hardly be expected to show a sharp, sustained interest in the abstractions of arithmetic, and the unrelated niceties of correct spelling. Punishment (or the threat of it) for this lack of interest is unlikely to bring the best out of him.'

While Mr Florian was speaking, something was happening to me. I had walked into his office full of high regard for him and ready to fall in with any plan he was likely to propose, but I found I was becoming increasingly irritated by his recital of the children's difficulties. My own experiences during the past two years invaded my thoughts, reminding me that these children were white; hungry or filled, naked or clothed, they were white, and as far as I was concerned, that fact alone made the only difference between the haves and the have-nots. I wanted this job badly and I was quite prepared to do it to the best of my ability, but it would be a job, not a labour of love.

'The next point I want to make,' he continued, 'deals with their conduct. You will soon discover that many of them smoke, use bad language and are often rather rude. We try our best to discourage these things without coercion, recognising that it is all part of the general malaise which affects the whole neighbourhood and produces a feeling of insecurity among the children. Instead, we try to give them affection, confidence and guidance, more or less in that order, because experience has shown us that those are their most immediate needs. Only a small part of their day is spent in the supervised security of this school; for the rest they may be exposed to many very unsatisfactory influences. A quick look round this neighbourhood will show that it is infested with a wide variety of social vermin, prostitutes, pimps, and perverts.'

I sat watching him, carefully attentive, impressed in spite of myself, by his deep, enthusiastic concern and undoubted love for the children. My irritation passed, but a feeling of doubt remained. He was speaking as if they were all tiny, helpless children, a description very much at variance with what I had seen of the husky youths and girls jiving in the auditorium. Evidently Mr Florian had the children's welfare very much at heart, but did he really believe all that he was saying about them – or was it all laid on for my benefit? Was every new applicant given this same sermon? Had Hackman received similar encouragement? I liked this man; his fervour and integrity gave him a stature which more than compensated for his lack of inches; his voice went on, deep, intense, spell-binding . . .

'It is said that here we practise free discipline. That's wrong, quite wrong. It would be more correct to say that we are seeking, as best we can, to establish disciplined freedom, that state in which the child feels free to work, play and express himself without fear of those whose job it is to direct and stimulate his efforts into constructive channels. As things are we cannot expect of them high academic effort, but we can take steps to ensure that their limited abilities are exploited to the full.' Here he smiled briefly, as if amused by some fleeting, private reflection. 'We encourage them to speak up for themselves, no matter what the circumstances or the occasion; this may probably take the form of rudeness at first but gradually, through the influences of the various Committees and the Student Council, we hope they will learn directness without rudeness, and humility without sycophancy. We try to show them a real relationship between themselves and their work, in preparation for the day when they leave school.

'As teachers, we can help greatly if we become sufficiently important to them; important enough for our influence to balance or even outweigh the evil.'

He got up and walked over to the large single window which overlooked the churchyard and remained there in silence for a while, his hands clasped behind his back, his leonine head resting against the cool glass. After a little while he turned to me with a gentle smile.

'Well, there it is. I'm afraid I can offer you no blueprint for teaching; it wouldn't work, especially here. From the moment you accept you're on your own. All the rest of the staff, myself included, will always be ready to help and advise if need be, but success or failure with them will depend entirely on you. So long as you work within the broad conceptual framework I have outlined, I shall not interfere. Unfortunately, we have had a number of teachers at one time or another who, though excellent in themselves, were totally unsuited for this type of work; and, as you'll appreciate, too frequent changes of staff neither help the children nor advance our work. Anyway, on behalf of the school and staff, I welcome you. You will have charge of the top class, beginning tomorrow, and will share the boys' P.T. periods with the other men on the staff. Mrs Drew, my deputy, will give you all the relevant information you need. I would suggest that you spend the afternoon finding your way about.'

He came towards me, hands outstretched. I rose, and he took my right hand in both his own with a firm, friendly grip.

'Remember,' he said, 'they're wonderful children when you get to know them, and somehow, I think you will. Good luck.'

I left him and wandered back to the staffroom. They all looked up enquiringly at my entry. Mrs Dale-Evans closed her newspaper and said:

'Well, what's the score?'

'I'm taking over Mr Hackman's class tomorrow,' I replied.

'And may the Lord God have mercy on your poor soul,' Weston intoned with mock solemnity.

'Lucky girls,' chirped Miss Clintridge. 'Along comes a man at last and they cop him all to themselves.'

27

'Don't look now, Clinty, but your psyche is showing all over the place.' Weston's hollow voice pushed its way through the hedge of reddish beard; there was no noticeable movement of his lips. But Clinty's Cockney humour was equal to his barb.

'It always does whenever there's a man around.' The emphasis she put on the word 'man' was devastating.

As the bell sounded for class, Mrs Drew came over to me and offered to brief me on the routine of registration, the collection of dinner money, and other duties which I would be expected to fulfil. I spent the afternoon, therefore, in her classroom, observing and admiring the skilful way in which she blended patience with firmness, order with bubbling activity. The youngsters were engaged at different tasks in small groups, resulting in a constant hum and buzz which I found somewhat irritating. I asked Mrs Drew about her reaction to it and she replied that she did not mind it; as long as they were busy they were learning, even though it seemed rather chaotic; and as they grew older they would see the need for greater concentration and quiet.

I remained with her until the bell sounded for the end of the school day.

On my way home that evening I felt an effervescence of spirit which built up inside me until I felt like shouting out loud for the sheer hell of it. The school, the children, Weston, the grimy fly-infested street through which I hurried – none of it could detract from the wonderful feeling of being employed. At long last I had a job, and though it promised to tax my capabilities to the full, it offered me the opportunity – wonderful word – of working on terms of dignified equality in an established profession.

Today I was a teacher, employed. True, I was also a teacher untried, but that could also be an advantage. I would learn, by God I'd learn. Nothing was going to stop me. Mrs Drew coped, Mrs Dale-Evans coped, Miss Clintridge coped, so I'd also cope, or bust. Four years ago I would not have even considered it possible. I did not become a teacher out of any sense of vocation; mine was no considered decision in the interests of youthful humanity or the spread of planned education. It was a decision forced on me by the very urgent need to eat; it was a decision brought about by a chain of unhappy experiences which began about a week after my demobilisation from the Royal Air Force in 1945.

CHAPTER 4

AT THE DEMOBILISATION Centre, after the usual round of Medical inspection, return of Service equipment, and issue of allowances and civilian clothing, I had been interviewed by an officer whose job it was to advise on careers. On learning that I had a science degree and varied experience in engineering technology, he expressed the opinion that I would have no difficulty in finding a good civilian job. Industry was re-organising itself for post-war production and there was already an urgent demand for qualified technologists, especially in the field of electronics, which was my special interest. I had been very much encouraged by this, as I had made a point of keeping up with new trends and developments by borrowing books through the Central Library System, and by subscribing to various technical journals and magazines, so I felt quite confident of my ability to hold down a good job. He had given me a letter of introduction to the Higher Appointments Office in Tavistock Square, London, and suggested that I call on them as soon as I had settled myself in 'digs' and had enjoyed a short holiday.

While operating from the R.A.F. Station at Hornchurch in Essex during the war, I had met and been frequently entertained by an elderly couple who lived not far away at Brentwood; I had kept in touch with them ever since and had promised to stay with them after demobilisation. I now went to live with them, and soon felt completely at home and at peace. They both professed to be atheists, but, judging by their conduct, they exhibited in their daily lives all those attributes which are fundamental to real, active Christianity. They were thoughtful for my comfort in every way, and shared many of my interests and pursuits with a zest which might well have been envied by much younger people. Together we went down to Torquay for a two-week holiday and returned to Brentwood completely refreshed.

Shortly after our return, I visited the Appointments Office, where I was interviewed by two courteous, impersonal men who questioned me closely on my academic background, service career and experience in industry. I explained that after graduating I had worked for two years as a Communications Engineer for the Standard Oil Company at their Aruba Refinery, earning enough to pay for post-graduate study in England. At the end of the interview they told me that I would be notified of any vacancies suitable to my experience and qualifications. Two weeks later I received a letter from the Appointments Office, together with a list of three firms, each of which had vacancies for qualified Communications Engineers. I promptly wrote to each one, stating my qualifications and experience, and soon received very encouraging replies, each with an invitation to an interview. Everything was working very smoothly and I felt on top of the world.

I was nervous as I stood in front of the Head Office in Mayfair; this firm had a high international reputation and the thought of being associated with it added to my excitement. Anyway, I reasoned, this was the first of the interviews, and if I boobed here there were still two chances remaining. The uniformed commissionaire courteously opened the large doors for me, and as I approached the receptionist's desk she smiled quite pleasantly.

'Good morning.' Her brows were raised in polite enquiry.

'Good morning,' I replied. 'My name is Braithwaite. I am here for an interview with Mr Symonds.'

I had taken a great deal of care with my appearance that morning. I was wearing my best suit with the right shirt and tie and pocket handkerchief; my shoes were smartly polished, my teeth were well brushed and I was wearing my best smile

– all this had passed the very critical inspection of Mr and Mrs Belmont with whom I lived. I might even say that I was quite proud of my appearance. Yet the receptionist's smile suddenly wavered and disappeared. She reached for a large diary and consulted it as if to verify my statement, then she picked up the telephone and, cupping her hand around the mouthpiece as if for greater privacy, spoke rapidly into it, watching me furtively the while.

'Will you come this way?' She set off down a wide corridor, her back straight and stiff with a disapproval which was echoed in the tap-tap of her high heels. As I walked behind her I thought: normally she'd be swinging it from side to side; now it's stiff with anger.

At the end of the corridor we entered an automatic lift: the girl maintained a silent hostility and avoided looking at me. At the second floor we stepped out into a passage on to which several rooms opened; pausing briefly outside one of them she said 'In there', and quickly retreated to the lift. I knocked on the door and entered a spacious room where four men were seated at a large table.

One of them rose, walked around to shake hands with me and introduced his colleagues, and then indicated a chair in which I seated myself. After a brief enquiry into my place of birth and R.A.F. service experience, they began to question me closely on telecommunications and the development of electronics in that field. The questions were studied, deliberate, and suddenly the nervousness which had plagued me all the morning disappeared; now I was confident, at ease with a familiar subject. They questioned me on theory, equipment, circuits, operation; on my training in the U.S.A., and on my experience there and in South America. They were thorough, but I was relaxed now; the years of study, field work and post-graduate research were about to pay off, and I knew that I was holding my own, and even enjoying it.

And then it was all over. Mr Symonds, the gentleman who had welcomed me, leaned back in his chair and looked from one to another of his associates. They nodded to him, and he said:

'Mr Braithwaite, my associates and I are completely satisfied with your replies and feel sure that in terms of qualification, ability and experience, you are abundantly suited to the post we have in mind. But we are faced with a certain difficulty. Employing you would mean placing you in a position of authority over a number of our English employees, many of whom have been with us a very long time, and we feel that such an appointment would adversely affect the balance of good relationship which has always obtained in this firm. We could not offer you that post without the responsibility, neither would we ask you to accept the one or two other vacancies of a different type which do exist, for they are unsuitable for someone with your high standard of education and ability. So, I'm afraid, we will not be able to use you.' At this he rose, extending his hand in the courtesy of dismissal.

I felt drained of strength and thought; yet somehow I managed to leave that office, navigate the passage, lift and corridor, and walk out of the building into the busy sunlit street. I had just been brought face to face with something I had either forgotten or completely ignored for more than six exciting years – my black skin. It had not mattered when I volunteered for aircrew service in 1940, it had not mattered during the period of flying training or when I received my wings and was posted to a squadron; it had not mattered in the hectic uncertainties of operational flying, of living and loving from day to day, brothered to men who like myself had no tomorrow and could not afford to fritter away today on the absurdities of prejudice; it had not mattered when, uniformed and winged, I visited theatres and dance-halls, pubs and private houses.

I had forgotten about my black face during those years. I saw it daily yet never noticed its colour. I was an airman in flying kit while on His Majesty's business, smiled at, encouraged, welcomed by grateful civilians in bars or on the street, who saw not me, but the uniform and its relationship to the glorious, undying Few. Yes, I had forgotten about my skin when I had so eagerly discussed my post-war prospects with the Careers Officer and the Appointments people; I had quite forgotten about it as I jauntily entered that grand, imposing building. . . .

Now, as I walked sadly away, I consciously averted my eyes from the sight of my face reflected fleetingly in the large plate glass shop windows. Disappointment and resentment were a solid bitter rising lump inside me; I hurried into the nearest public lavatory and was violently sick.

Relieved, I walked about, somewhat aimlessly, and tried to pull myself together. The more I thought of it the more I realised that the whole interview had been a waste of time. They had agreed on their decision before I had walked into that office; the receptionist had told them about my black face, and all that followed had been a cruel, meaningless charade. I stopped suddenly, struck by a new realisation. Those folk must have looked at my name on the application forms and immediately assumed that I was white; there was nothing about the name Braithwaite to indicate my colour, so the flowery letters and pleasant invitation to interview were really intended for the white applicant they imagined me to be. God, how they must have hated me for the trick I had so unwittingly played on them!

Acting on a sudden impulse, I went into a telephone booth and in turn called the two remaining firms. I explained that I wanted to let them know that I was a Negro, but would be very happy to attend for the interview if my colour was no barrier to possible employment. In each case I was thanked for telephoning, but informed that the post had already been filled and it had been their intention to write me to that effect. So that was that. Angered and disgusted, I caught a train to take me as quickly as possible to the only place in all Britain where I knew I would feel safe and wanted – the Belmont home in Brentwood.

Belief in an ideal dies hard. I had believed in an ideal for all the twenty-eight years of my life – the ideal of the British Way of Life.

It had sustained me when as a youth in a high school of nearly all white students I had had to work harder or run faster than they needed to do in order to make the grade. It had inspired me in my college and university years when ideals were dragged in the dust of disillusionment following the Spanish Civil War. Because of it I had never sought to acquire American citizenship, and when, after graduation and two years of field work in Venezuela, I came to England for post-graduate study in 1939, I felt that at long last I was personally identified with the hub of fairness, tolerance and all the freedoms. It was therefore without any hesitation that I volunteered for service with the Royal Air Force in 1940, willing and ready to lay down my life for the preservation of the ideal which had been my lodestar. But now that self-same ideal was gall and wormwood in my mouth.

The majority of Britons at home have very little appreciation of what that intangible yet amazingly real and invaluable export – the British Way of Life – means to colonial people; and they seem to give little thought to the fantastic phenomenon of races so very different from themselves in pigmentation, and widely scattered geographically, assiduously identifying themselves with British loyalties, beliefs and traditions. This attitude can easily be observed in the way in which the coloured Colonial will quote the British systems of Law, Education and Government, and will adopt fashions in dress and social codes, even though his knowledge of these things has depended largely on secondhand information. All this is especially true of the West Indian Colonials, who are predominantly the descendants of slaves who were forever removed from the cultural influence of their forefathers, and who lived, worked, and reared their children through the rigours of slavery and the growing pains of gradual enfranchisement, according to the only example they knew – the British Way.

The ties which bind them to Britain are strong, and this is very apparent on each occasion of a Royal visit, when all of them, young and old, rich and poor, join happily together in unrestrained and joyful demonstrations of welcome. Yes, it is wonderful to be British – until one comes to Britain. By dint of careful saving or through hard-won scholarships many of them arrive in Britain to be educated in the Arts and Sciences and in the varied processes of legislative and administrative government. They come, bolstered by a firm, conditioned belief that Britain and the British stand for all that is best in both Christian and Democratic terms; in their naïveté they ascribe these high principles to all Britons, without exception.

I had grown up British in every way. Myself, my parents and my parents' parents, none of us knew or could know any other way of living, of thinking, of being; we knew no other cultural pattern, and I had never heard any of my forebears complain about being British. As a boy I was taught to appreciate English literature, poetry and prose, classical and contemporary, and it was absolutely natural for me to identify myself with the British heroes of the adventure stories against the villains of the piece who were invariably non-British and so, to my boyish mind, more easily capable of villainous conduct. The more selective reading of my college and university life was marked by the same predilection for English literature, and I did not hesitate to defend my preferences to my American colleagues. In fact, all the while in America, I vigorously resisted any criticism of Britain or British policy, even when in the privacy of my own room, closer examination clearly proved the reasonableness of such criticism.

It is possible to measure with considerable accuracy the rise and fall of the tides, or the behaviour in space of objects invisible to the naked eye. But who can measure the depths of disillusionment? Within the somewhat restricted sphere of an academic institution, the Colonial student learns to heal, debate, to paint and to think; outside that sphere he has to meet the indignities and rebuffs of intolerance, prejudice and hate. After qualification and establishment in practice or position, the trials and successes of academic life are half forgotten in the hurly-burly of living, but the hurts are not so easily forgotten. Who can predict the end result of a land-lady's coldness, a waiter's discourtesy, or the refusal of a young woman to dance? The student of today may be the Prime Minister of tomorrow. Might not some future important political decision be influenced by a remembered slight or festering resentment? Is it reasonable to expect that those sons of Nigeria, the Gold Coast, the West Indies, British Guiana, Honduras, Malaya, Ceylon, Hong Kong and others who are constitutionally agitating for self-government, are completely unaffected by experiences of intolerance suffered in Britain and elsewhere?

To many in Britain a Negro is a 'darky' or a 'nigger' or a 'black'; he is identified, in their minds, with inexhaustible brute strength; and often I would hear the remark 'working like a nigger' or 'labouring like a black' used to emphasise some occasion of sustained effort. They expect of him a courteous subservience and contentment with a lowly state of menial employment and slum accommodation. It is true that here and there one sees Negroes as doctors, lawyers or talented entertainers, but they are somehow considered 'different' and not to be confused with the mass.

I am a Negro, and what had happened to me at that interview constituted, to my mind, a betrayal of faith. I had believed in freedom, in the freedom to live in the kind of dwelling I wanted, providing I was able and willing to pay the price; and in the freedom to work at the kind of profession for which I was qualified, without reference to my racial or religious origins. All the big talk of Democracy and Human Rights seemed as spurious as the glib guarantees with which some manufacturers underwrite their products in the confident hope that they will never be challenged. The Briton at home takes no responsibility for the protestations and promises made in his name by British officials overseas.

I reflected on my life in the U.S.A. There, when prejudice is felt, it is open, obvious, blatant; the white man makes his position very clear, and the black man fights those prejudices with equal openness and fervour, using every constitutional device available to him. The rest of the world in general and Britain in particular are prone to point an angrily critical finger at American intolerance, forgetting that in its short history as a nation it has granted to its Negro citizens more opportunities for advancement and betterment, *per capita*, than any other nation in the world with an indigent Negro population. Each violent episode, though greatly to be deplored, has invariably preceded some change, some improvement in the American Negro's position. The things they have wanted were important enough for them to fight and die for, and those who died did not give their lives in vain. Furthermore, American Negroes have been generally established in communities in which their abilities as labourer, artisan, doctor, lawyer, scientist, educator and entertainer have been directly or indirectly of benefit to that community; in terms of social and religious intercourse they have been largely independent of white people.

In Britain I found things to be very different. I have yet to meet a single English person who has actually admitted to anti-Negro prejudice; it is even generally believed that no such thing exists here. A Negro is free to board any bus or train and sit anywhere, provided he has paid the appropriate fare; the fact that many people might pointedly avoid sitting near to him is casually overlooked. He is free to seek accommodation in any licensed hotel or boarding house – the courteous refusal which frequently follows is never ascribed to prejudice. The betrayal I now felt was greater because it had been perpetrated with the greatest of charm and courtesy.

I realised at that moment that I was British, but evidently not a Briton, and that fine differentiation was now very important; I would need to re-examine myself and my whole future in terms of this new appraisal.

The war was over and I must forget that period; people were settling down once again to a pattern of life free from terror, and communal fears which had momentarily promoted communal virtues were evaporating in the excitement of economic recovery. I must find a job. I was not asking for handouts, but offering for hire a trained mind and healthy body. Surely there must be some employer who would be more interested in my trained usefulness to him than in the colour of my skin? My savings and gratuity would, with careful husbandry, last about two years. So I had time, plenty of time, to find the right employer.

CHAPTER 5

I TRIED EVERYTHING – labour exchanges, employment agencies, newspaper ads – all with the same result. I even advertised myself mentioning my qualifications and the colour of my skin, but there were no takers. Then I tried applying for jobs without mentioning my colour, but when they saw me the reasons given for turning me down were all variations of the same theme: too black.

There was, for instance, the electrical firm at Dagenham which advertised for technicians in a local newspaper. No special qualifications were indicated, so I applied, hopeful that my trained abilities would stand me in good stead; this time I did not mention my colour. I received a prompt reply, asking me to call at the personnel office the following morning. I presented myself there about 9.0 a.m. and a young female clerk handed me an application form and directed me to an ante-room where I had to fill it in and wait my turn to see the Personnel Manager.

Several young men were sitting there, some of them waiting nervously, others filling in their forms with worried concentration. One young man was unsure about his spelling and appealed to the others for assistance; they too were unsure, and I was pleased to be able to set him right.

One by one they were called away and then it was my turn. The Personnel Manager sat with my form on the desk before him; he indicated a chair, picked up the form and closely scrutinised it. We went through the familiar game of question and answer, and I soon realised that he did not seem very interested in the extent of my technical knowledge. Finally he said, with a grin, 'Why do you want this job?'

I felt somewhat irritated by the irrelevance of this remark and replied:

'I need the job to help me pay for little things like the food I eat, the clothes I wear and the lodgings I occupy.'

'Ha, I couldn't afford a suit like the one you're wearing.'

I watched him, failing to see any connection between my suit and the advertised job. He continued:

'I never went to Grammar school, let alone University, and none of our employees are as well educated as you are, so I don't think you'd fit in here. They might resent the posh way you speak and . . .'

I could stand no more but stood up, reached across his desk for the application form and, without a word, tore it up and carefully dropped the pieces into his waste basket. Then I bade him good morning and left.

I had now been jobless for nearly eighteen months. Disillusionment had given place to a deepening, poisoning hatred; slowly but surely I was hating these people who could so casually, so unfeelingly deny me the right to earn a living. I was considered too well educated, too good for the lowly jobs, and too black for anything better. Now, it seemed, they even resented the fact that I looked tidy.

When my demobilisation became imminent I had written to my uncle about the problem of clothes rationing, and, over a period of months, he had sent me a supply of underwear, shirts, socks, ties and four nice looking suits which fitted me tolerably well; the clothing coupons I had received at the demob centre were used in purchasing a few pairs of very serviceable shoes.

Caught like an insect in the tweezer grip of prejudice, I felt myself striking out in unreasoning retaliation. I became distrustful of every glance or gesture, seeking to probe behind them to expose the antipathy and intolerance which, I felt sure, was there. I was no longer disposed to extend to English women or elderly people on buses and trains those essential courtesies which, from childhood, I had accorded them as a rightful tribute, and even found myself glaring in undisguised hostility at small children whose innocently enquiring eyes were attracted by my unfamiliar complexion.

Fortunately for me, this cancerous condition was not allowed to establish itself firmly. Every now and then, and in spite of myself, some person or persons would say or do something so utterly unselfish and friendly that I would temporarily forget my difficulties and hurts. It was from such an unexpected quarter that I received the helpful advice which changed the whole course of my life.

I had been sitting beside the lake in St James's Park, idly watching the ducks as they dived for the bits of food thrown to them by passers-by. Near me was seated a thin, bespectacled old gentleman who occasionally commented on the colour or habits of the various species. He sounded quite knowledgeable, but I was in no mood for that sort of thing, and mentally dismissed him as just another garrulous old crank. He did not seem to mind my unresponsive attitude, however, and presently addressed me directly.

'Been in England long, young man?'

His voice had the same sandpapery grittiness as Bertrand Russell's, and I turned to look at him with what I hoped was a sufficiently cutting glance to discourage his overtures; I did not feel at all like conversation, especially on the very painful subject of being in England.

'Big cities are dreadfully lonely places and London is no exception.'

He hitched up his carefully creased trousers and crossed his thin legs. He wanted to talk; some old men are like that. It would not matter who had been sitting beside him. I did not need to reply or even to listen, and if I walked away he would very likely talk to the ducks. Anyway, I could not be bothered to move to another seat. When he got tired he'd stop.

'It's no one's fault, really,' he continued. 'A big city cannot afford to have its attention distracted from the important job of being a big city by such a tiny, unimportant item as your happiness or mine.'

This came out of him easily, assuredly, and I was suddenly

interested. On closer inspection there was something aesthetic and scholarly about him, something faintly professorial. He knew I was with him, listening, and his grey eyes were kind with offered friendliness. He continued:

'Those tall buildings there are more than monuments to the industry, thought and effort which have made this a great city; they also occasionally serve as springboards to eternity for misfits who cannot cope with the city and their own loneliness in it.' He paused and said something about one of the ducks which was quite unintelligible to me. 'A great city is a battlefield,' he continued. 'You need to be a fighter to live in it, not exist, mark you, live. Anybody can exist, dragging his soul around behind him like a worn-out coat; but living is different. It can be hard, but it can also be fun; there's so much going on all the time that's new and exciting.'

I could not, nor wished to, ignore his pleasant voice, but I was in no mood for his philosophising.

'If you were a Negro you'd find that even existing would provide more excitement than you'd care for.'

He looked at me and suddenly laughed; a laugh abandoned and gay, a laugh rich and young and indescribably infectious. I laughed with him, although I failed to see anything funny in my remark.

'I wondered how long it would be before you broke down and talked to me,' he said, when his amusement had quietened down. 'Talking helps, you know; if you can talk with someone you're not lonely any more, don't you think?'

As simple as that. Soon we were chatting away unreservedly, like old friends, and I had told him everything.

'Teaching,' he said presently. 'That's the thing. Why not get a job as a teacher?'

'That's rather unlikely,' I replied. 'I have had no training as a teacher.'

'Oh, that's not absolutely necessary. Your degrees would be considered in lieu of training, and I feel sure that with your experience and obvious ability you could do well.'

'Look here, Sir, if these people would not let me near

42

ordinary inanimate equipment about which I understand quite a bit, is it reasonable to expect them to entrust the education of their children to me?'

'Why not? They need teachers desperately.'

'It is said that they also need technicians desperately.'

'Ah, but that's different. I don't suppose Education Authorities can be bothered about the colour of people's skins, and I do believe that in that respect the London County Council is rather outstanding. Anyway, there would be no need to mention it; let it wait until they see you at the interview.'

'I've tried that method before. It didn't work.'

'Try it again, you've nothing to lose. I know for a fact that there are many vacancies for teachers in the East End of London.'

'Why especially the East End of London?'

'From all accounts it is rather a tough area, and most teachers prefer to seek jobs elsewhere.'

'And you think it would be just right for a Negro, I suppose.' The vicious bitterness was creeping back; the suspicion was not so easily forgotten.

'Now, just a moment, young man.' He was wonderfully patient with me, much more so than I deserved. 'Don't ever underrate the people of the East End; from those very slums and alleyways are emerging many of the new breed of professional and scientific men and quite a few of our politicians. Be careful lest you be a worse snob than the rest of us. Was this the kind of spirit in which you sought the other jobs?'

I felt that I had angered him, and apologised; I was showing poor appreciation of his kind interest.

'Anyway, you try it. No need to mention your colour at this stage, first see how the cat jumps.'

Once more I was at ease with him, and talked with pleasure about many things. It was only after we had parted that I realised we had spent over two hours in very rewarding discussion without being introduced: we had not even exchanged names. I hope that he may one day read these pages and know how deeply grateful I am for that timely and fateful meeting.

It happened just as he had predicted. I was invited to the Ministry of Education for an interview, and later a letter arrived informing me that I would be accepted subject to a satisfactory medical examination. That hurdle safely cleared, I received a final letter confirming my appointment and directing me to call at the East London Divisional Office; and from there I was sent on to Greenslade School.

CHAPTER 6

I ARRIVED EARLY for class my first day as a teacher at Greenslade School. The joy and excitement I felt at my good fortune was shared in equal measure by the Belmonts with whom I lived, and whom I had always called 'Dad' and 'Mom' at their own suggestion. As I was leaving home that morning, Mom had, with sudden impulse, kissed me at the door and wished me 'Best of Luck', while Dad looked on, less demonstrative, but just as happy for me. I walked off feeling very strong, confident, and determined to make good.

As I entered the narrow alleyway leading to the school I could hear the strident voices of the early children in the playground; one girlish voice was raised in violent protest.

'Denham, why don't you let the f——ing netball alone?'

Shocked, I walked into the forecourt, which was used as a playground, and saw a group of girls spaced around a netball standard; one of them held a netball behind her back, away from a big, loutish fellow who had interposed himself between her and the net into which she wanted to throw it.

'Move out the bloody way, youse, or I'll. . .'

At this point they heard my approach and looked around, but seeing me made little difference for, as I mounted the stairs, I could hear their voices again, brutally frank in Anglo-Saxon references. Confidence began to ooze out of me; would they actually use words like that in the classroom? The idea was fantastic.

Mrs Drew was sitting in the staffroom reading her newspaper. I greeted her and removed my overcoat.

'All set for the fray?' Her voice was soft, sympathetic.

'I think so. Mrs Drew, do the children use bad language inside the school, in the classrooms?'

'Sometimes.' There was always a gravity behind her remarks, indicative of a really deep concern for the children, and a certain objective examination of her own efforts on their behalf. 'Most of the time they are merely showing off; the words themselves are not in their minds associated with the acts they suggest, and it is often good policy to behave as if one did not hear. Some of the older ones deliberately set out to shock, to offend. I get very little of it these days – I suppose out of deference to my grey hairs.' She patted her neat coiffure. 'I'm afraid I cannot tell you how to deal with it, you'll just have to do the best you can.'

One by one the staff arrived and soon there was a pleasing interchange of chatter until the morning bell rang.

As I was leaving the room I looked across at Miss Blanchard and she smiled her encouragement; Miss Clintridge called out cheerily 'Good luck.'

From outside the classroom I could hear sounds of talk, laughter and movement. I went in and walked directly to my desk, seated myself and waited. The children were standing about in groups and had paid no attention to my entrance; but gradually, the groups dispersed and they seated themselves. I waited until everyone was quietly settled, then called the attendance register.

Their replies to their names were mostly mumbles or grunts, with here or there a 'yep' or 'here'. One boy answered 'Here, Sir', and this promptly provoked a chorus of jeers from boys and girls alike, in resentment at his black-legging their agreed action.

Next, I collected the dinner money. The institution of school dinners is a real boon to both children and parents; for prices ranging from eightpence to threepence, depending upon the number of children of school age in the family, the child receives a hot midday meal, well-balanced and satisfying; and with the blessing of the local Child Care Committee it is free to those who are unable to pay even these small amounts. Mrs Drew had assured me that the robust huskiness of the children was largely due to the school meals and free mid-morning milk; but that, surprisingly, some of the children preferred to use their dinner money to buy packets of chips from a nearby fish shop. Habits are not easily forgotten.

Registration over, I sat back to take my first careful look at the class before we were summoned into the auditorium for daily assembly. A quick count revealed forty-six positions, forty-two of which were occupied. They were set in four straight lines and from my desk I commanded a clear view of them all. Twenty-six of the class were girls, and many of their faces bore traces of make-up inexpertly or hurriedly removed, giving to their obvious youth a slightly tawdry, jaded look: these were really young women who sat there, quiet and watchful, gypsyish in their flashy cheap earrings and bracelets.

The boys were scruffier, coarser, dirtier, everything about them indicated a planned conformity – the T-shirts, jeans, haircuts, the same wary sullenness. None of it really belonged to them. It was worn, assumed in and out of school like a kind of armour; a gesture against authority; a symbol of toughness as thin and synthetic as the cheap films from which it was copied.

I had begun to feel a bit uneasy under their silent, concentrated appraisal when the bell rang and they eagerly trooped out into the auditorium for assembly.

The Headmaster sat in the centre of a stage at one end of the hall. This stage was the show-piece of the school. Under Miss Clintridge's direction, what had been a bare, simple platform was now a thing of elegance, with a gay proscenium, and curtain decorated in contemporary style; the backdrop represented a bustling local market scene, and the whole effect was familiar, gay and vigorous. Near him sat a girl whose task it was to select and play the two records which were part of the proceedings – usually orchestral selections from classical works, or vocal recordings by outstanding artists like Paul Robeson, Maria Callas, Marian Anderson and others. In this way it was hoped to widen their musical interest beyond the jazz and boogie-woogie offerings of the midday dance sessions.

The children sat in rows facing the stage and the teachers sat in line behind them; Assembly was a simple affair without religious bias or emphasis. It began with a hymn and prayer in which every child joined, either actively, or merely by being there. Jew and Gentile, Catholic and Protestant and Moslem, they were all there, all in it, all of it; the invocation for guidance, courage and Divine help was for each and all.

After the prayer the Head read a poem, *La Belle Dame Sans Merci*. The records which followed were Chopin's *Fantaisie Impromptu*, and part of Vivaldi's *Concerto in C* for two trumpets. They listened, those rough looking, untidy children; every one of them sat still, unmoving and attentive, until the very echo of the last clear note had died away. Their silence was not the result of boredom or apathy, nor were they quiet because it was expected of them or through fear of consequences; but they were listening, actively, attentively listening to those records, with the same raptness they had shown in their jiving; their bodies were still, but I could feel that their minds and spirits were involved with the music. I glanced towards Miss Blanchard and as though she divined my thoughts she smiled at me and nodded in understanding.

After the records the Headmaster introduced me to the school. He simply told them that a new teacher, Mr Braithwaite, had joined the staff and would be teaching Class 4; he felt sure that they all joined him and the staff in bidding me welcome.

In the classroom I stood in front of my desk and waited until they were settled, then I said:

'The Headmaster has told you my name, but it will be some little while before I know all yours, so in the meantime I hope you won't mind if I point at you or anything like that; it will not be meant rudely.' I tried to inject as much pleasant informality as possible into my voice. 'I do not know anything about you or your abilities, so I will begin from scratch. One by one I'll listen to you reading; when I call your name will you please read anything you like from any one of your schoolbooks.'

I sat down, opened the Attendance register and called one name at random. 'Palmer, will you read for us, please.'

I followed the gaze of the class and discovered that Palmer was a red-faced, bull-necked boy, with pale eyes and a very large close-cropped head.

'Will you stand up, please?'

He looked around the class indecisively, then rose to his feet and began to read slowly, haltingly.

'That will do, Palmer. Now, Benjamin, will you carry on?'

Palmer sat down, looking at me questioningly. His reading was shockingly bad. Benjamin's effort was not much better, nor was that of Sapiano, Wells or Drake.

'Jane Purcell, will you read, please.'

The girl who rose to comply was fair-haired and slim, with a pair of heavy breasts which swung loosely under a thin jumper, evidently innocent of any support. I wondered at the kind of parent who would allow a girl to go out so sloppily attired. She read better than the others, that is to say she recognised more words, but they were disconnected from each other in a way which robbed them of much of their meaning.

While the Purcell girl read I noticed that there was some laughter and inattention among some of the children at the back of the class. Without interrupting the reader, I rose quietly and went to investigate. One of the boys, the same big fellow who had been annoying the girls earlier that morning, was playing with or demonstrating something behind the raised flap of his desk, and his immediate neighbours were helpless with suppressed laughter.

Unobserved I reached him and felt a wave of disgust as I saw what he held in his hand. It was a female figure in flesh-coloured rubber, poised straddle-legged on a small globe; as he pressed the globe between finger and thumb the flaccidly concave breasts and abdomen leaped into exaggeratedly inflated relief and presented a picture of lewdly advanced pregnancy.

'Will you put that away please?'

He casually put the figure in his pocket, favouring me the while with a cool, insolent stare; then he pulled his hand away from the desk and let the lid fall back into place with a loud bang. The girl stopped reading, and I knew they were all watching me, tense and anxious. Anger was rising in me, filling my throat; but somehow I managed to hold myself in check. I walked back to my desk. Keep calm, I said to myself, you've got to keep calm.

'Potter, will you read, please?'

Potter was tall and very fat, easily the largest boy in the class. He read reasonably well, and when I raised my hand for him to stop, he beamed happily.

'Sit down, Potter.' My voice was sharp. 'I take it you would all agree that this book is written in English, your language and that of your ancestors. After listening to you, I am not sure whether you are reading badly deliberately, or are unable to understand or express your own language. However, it may be that I have done you the injustice of selecting the worst readers. Would anyone else like to read for me?'

There was a pause, then a hand shot up at the farthest end of the back row. It belonged to the red-head whom I had encountered the day before. I noticed that unlike most of the class she was clean and neat.

'Your name, please?'

'Dare, Pamela Dare.'

'Begin, please.'

It was a passage from Louis Stevenson's *Treasure Island* . . .

' "In I got bodily into the apple barrel and found there scarce an apple left . . . ." '

Her voice was clear, warm and well-modulated; she read easily, flowing the words into a clear picture of the boy's terrifying experience. The passage ended, she stopped and looked at me defiantly, as if satisfied with this vindication of her colleagues, then abruptly sat down.

'Thank you, Pamela Dare. Anyone else like to try?'

No one offered, so I spoke to them at some length about reading, emphasising that it was the most important of the basic skills they were expected to master. Occasionally I walked over to a desk at random, picked up a book, and read from it to illustrate some point I was making. They sat watching me, quietly, ominously, but they were listening, and I warmed to my subject, primarily concerned with keeping them that way. The bell for recess was a very welcome sound, and they trooped out to their mid-morning milk while I sat down at my desk to give some further thought to the next lesson.

There was a knock on the door and Miss Clintridge came in carrying two cups of tea, one of which she placed on my desk. I stood up, but she airily waved the courtesy aside and perched herself on one side of my desk.

'Thought you'd like a cuppa. How did it go, ducks?'

'Oh, not too badly, I think; one of the boys was a bit of a nuisance.' I told her of the incident.

'What did you do with it?'

'Oh, I didn't take it from him, I told him to put it away.'

She gave me a long searching look over the rim of her teacup, then she said:

'By the way, what's your name?'

'Braithwaite.'

'Not that, silly, your other name.'

'Ricky; you know, short for Ricardo.'

'Mine's Vivienne, but everyone calls me Clinty.'

'Suits you. Sharp.'

'So I've been told. Now look here, Ricky, there are one or two things I think you ought to understand. We all know the Old Man's views and ideas about teaching these kids, and we agree with them. But there's another side to it; the Old Man's views are wonderful when considered from the safety of his office, but in the classrooms we have to try to put these views into effect, and that's a different kettle of fish. Now look at it from the children's point of view; they come from homes where an order is invariably accompanied by a blow, and they do what they're told or else. They might use bad language to their friends, but if they try it on their parents or older brothers or sisters they get a clip on the ear. Well, they come here and soon discover that no blows are flying about and that they can say and do as they please. So what happens? Little Alfie or Mary takes that as licence to say anything he or she likes, and the poor teacher has to stand there and take it; and the more you take from them, the worse it gets. Right?'

'Right.'

'Well, we've got ourselves to consider as well as the kids. It's up to us to make our work bearable, so take a tip from me. Don't touch them, especially the girls, don't lay a finger on them or the next thing you know they'll be screaming high and low that you were interfering with them – but at the same time find some way of making them know who's boss. We've all had to. They're scared of Grace, and they've a great respect for Selma Drew's tongue – she may look as if she wouldn't say "boo" to a goose, but when she's roused she's a real bitch.

'Me, I was born around hereabouts and they know it, so I can give as good as I get. Don't take any guff from them, Ricky, or they'll give you hell. Sit heavily on them at first; then, if they play ball, you can always ease up. That ass Hackman tried to be popular with this lot; he gave them too much rope and they used it to hang him; served the cranky bastard right.' She paused long enough to finish her tea. 'Your tea's getting cold, Rick.'

She hopped down from the desk. 'Remember, don't take any crap from them, any of them.' She picked up the two cups and was gone, as bright and gusty as a May breeze.

'Thank you, Clinty, I'll remember.'

Before the class returned I set up the blackboard on its easel and waited for them, somewhat impatiently. As soon as they were settled once more I began.

'Our arithmetic lesson will be on weights and measures. As with our reading lesson, I am again trying to find out how much you know about it and you can help by answering my questions as fully as you are able. Does anyone know the table of weights, Avoirdupois?'

'Aver er what?'

'Avoirdupois,' I repeated, hoping my pronunciation of the word was correct. 'It refers to those weights commonly used in grocers' shops and the like.'

'Yeah, I know.' The thickset fellow was slumped low in his chair. 'Like heavyweight, light-heavy, cruiserweight, middle, light bantam, flyweight, featherweight.'

He held up both hands like a toddler in kindergarten and was playfully counting off on his fingers. When he stopped they laughed, and at that he stood up and bowed to them with mock gravity. It was really very funny, and in another place, at another time, I, too, would have laughed as uproariously as the rest. But, for good or ill, this was my classroom, and Clinty's words were still echoing in my ear. I let the laughter run its course. I folded my arms across my chest and leaned against my desk until every last one of them had laughed his fill and subsided. Then:

'What's your name, please?' I was angry and my voice was brittle.

'Denham.'

'Well, Denham, that's one way of applying the table of weights. Are you interested in boxing, Denham?'

'Yeah.' He flexed his shoulders and gazed lazily around the room.

'I see. Well, if you have at least learned to apply the table in that limited respect, it cannot be said that you are altogether stupid, can it, Denham?'

The smile left his face.

'Is there anyone else who would like to say something about the table of weights?'

'Tons, hundredweights, quarters, pounds, ounces.' The voice came suddenly from just in front of me. I looked into the upturned face of the little fellow of yesterday's cigarette incident.

'Yes, that's correct. What's your name, please?'

'Tich, Tich Jackson.'

I felt rather pleased at this gesture of co-operation.

'In some places, like the U.S.A. and the West Indies, although they use this same table of weights, they refer to pounds or tons, but never to stones or hundredweights. So a man would speak of his weight as 170 pounds, while here in England it would be 12 stone, 2 pounds, which would put him in the cruiserweight class, I suppose.'

'Welterweight.' Denham's tone was casual but authoritative.

'Thank you, Denham, welterweight. There are other weights in use. Troy weight is used by jewellers in weighing precious metals like gold, silver or platinum.'

'Diamonds are a girl's best friend.'

A loud roar of laughter followed this remark. I was not sure who was responsible, but I knew it came from the back row. I looked at Denham but he returned my gaze levelly, even insolently.

'Don't care for them much meself.'

A stout, sallow-skinned girl removed the necklace of coloured glass beads from her rather grimy neck with an elaborate gesture and held them up for general inspection.

'Pearls is more in my line.'

Her mimicry and exaggerated gestures held the class helpless with laughter.

I knew that I had to do something, anything, and quickly. They were challenging my authority, probably with no feeling of antipathy to myself, but merely to maintain a kind of established convention of resistance to a new teacher, watching closely for any sign of weakness or indecision. Maybe this was what Clinty was really hinting at. Okay, if a fight was what they wanted. . . . 'That's enough!' My voice was sharp and loud, cutting off their laughter. 'I find it both interesting and encouraging to discover that you have a sense of humour, especially about something as simple and elementary as weights. As a matter of fact, you seem to find everything rather amusing. You were amused at your inability to read simple passages in your own language, and now you are amused at your ignorance of weights. Many folk I have met have been disturbed, even distressed at their lack of knowledge; in your case you find such a lack amusing.' I was being sarcastic, deliberately, incisively sarcastic. 'It is therefore very clear to me that we shall have a most delightful time together; you seem to know so very little, and you are so easily amused, that I can look forward to a very happy time.'

There were murmurs of 'bleeding cheek' from some of them. They were not smiling now, but glaring angrily at me. This was much better.

'Now we'll turn our attention to measurements, beginning with linear measurement. Do you know the table of linear measurement, Denham?'

'Don't know what you mean.'

'Well, before I explain I'll wait until you've all had the usual laugh.'

They remained grave, angry, watchful.

'Does anyone else know the table I'm referring to?'

'Inches, feet, yards, furlongs, miles.' It was the fat, freckled girl who spoke.

'Yes, that's quite correct. It's called linear because it is concerned with lines.'

I then began to give them some background history on measurement and the way in which it affected the daily lives of all of us. They listened, and I kept them listening until the dinner bell rang.

CHAPTER 7

I DID NOT go to the dining hall for lunch. I had not enjoyed my meal there the previous day, as I found the bang and clatter a source of irritation. So Mom had fixed me up a lunch pack with sandwiches and an apple, and I went up to the staffroom to lunch in peace. I felt surprisingly spent, and realised with something of a shock that teaching imposed a great deal more strain than I had imagined.

Soon after I had settled down Miss Blanchard came in.

'Oh, hello, don't you like the food either?' She sat down and began to unwrap a packet of sandwiches.

'I suppose the food is okay, but I don't care for the noise.'

'The food's too stodgy for me, so I either bring along some of these, or if I'm in the mood I go across to a Kosher restaurant near by. It looks rather dingy on the outside, but it's very clean and the food's good.'

We soon fell into easy, pleasant conversation, and discovered a common interest in books, music, the theatre and films.

'You seemed surprised this morning.'

'Me, surprised, why?'

'In assembly. I never would have believed either that they'd even listen let alone enjoy classical music.'

'Don't you think it might have been those records, especially the Concerto for two trumpets? It was rather dominating, you know.'

'Perhaps, but in the few days I've been here it's been the same each time and the records have always been different.'

'Amazing, truly amazing.'

'How did it go today?'

I gave her a résumé of the morning's events.

'Good Lord. Maybe Weston was right, after all.'

'Too early to say. Anyway I think I'll do as Clinty, Miss Clintridge, suggests.'

'Oh, has she taken you under her wing?'

I looked at her but could read nothing in her smiling face.

'Not really, but if that's the way to cope with them, I'll try it.'

One by one the others returned from their lunch, and I was asked about the morning's progress.

'Don't be too hard on them,' Mrs Drew cautioned. 'They mean no harm, really; they're not bad when you get to know them.'

I remembered what Clinty had told me about her and smiled to myself.

'The trick is getting to know them.' Weston's hollow squeaky voice filtered its way through the untidy growth which nearly hid his mouth. It occurred to me that a quick pull on one whisker would cause the whole beard to unravel like an old jumper, leaving his face as naked as the backside of a plucked chicken.

'Do you know them?' Clinty's voice was sugary; she seemed to like baiting him.

'They do what I tell them in class and that's all I ask.'

'And that's about all you'll get, Big Boy.'

'They're not as black as they're painted.' Miss Dawes' prim mouth formed each word carefully. She was sitting in a corner beside Miss Phillips; they were always together, always whispering their unending secrets. Miss Dawes surprised me, every time I looked at her. Those large, round breasts seemed completely out of character with the brogue shoes, the ankle socks and the severe, naked lips; it was as though they were on the wrong person.

'Nobody's been painting them, Ducky, that's dirt.'

Grace passed the teacups around.

'Oh, you know what I mean.'

'Sure I know what you mean, but you don't know what I mean. You should listen in to some of their conversations when they're sitting together at needlework; make your hair curl, it would. You couldn't paint those little darlings if you tried.'

'Maybe Braithwaite will try a little black magic on them?' Weston just had to have his two cents worth.

No sale, no bid. I couldn't make up my mind about Weston, just how much was meant by the things he said. He seemed to delight in being irritating, yet always with a smile on his face. Certain recent experiences had left some very raw areas on my spirit and I suspected I might be unnecessarily sensitive. I also had the feeling that the day he really got under my skin I'd flatten him; so to be on the safe side I decided I'd just not hear the things he said. For all I knew the fellow was really trying to be friendly in an involved sort of way. I'd been a long while getting a job, and I was not prepared to throw it over for someone like him.

'What kind of magic do *you* try, Weston?' Mrs Drew's voice was cold. Clinty was right; she could be a bitch, a real bitch. Weston looked at her, apparently decided against replying, and fell into a broody silence.

I looked at Miss Blanchard and she grinned conspiratorially. This much was clear, most of my colleagues wanted me to make good; they had accepted me unconditionally as one of them. And that was the most important thing of all.

The afternoon's lessons passed without incident, but unsatisfactorily. The children neither chatted nor laughed, nor in any way challenged my authority, but at the same time they were uncooperative. They listened to me, or did the tasks assigned to them, like automata. My attempts at pleasantries were received with a chilly lack of response which indicated that my earlier remarks had got under their skin. Their silent watchfulness was getting under mine.

Not all of them, however. Tich Jackson seemed disposed to be friendly from the beginning, and though he had joined with the others in their laughter, whenever I looked at him he would smile, naturally. Another one who showed no resentment was Patrick Fernman, a thin-faced intelligent boy whose dark cowlick was always getting in his eyes. One other member of the class excited my curiosity. He was a well-built dark-skinned boy obviously of mixed parentage named Seales, Lawrence Seales. He never spoke unless addressed directly, and though dressed in the same T-shirt and jeans uniform as his colleagues, he seemed somehow aloof, taking no part in their ribaldry; and yet he showed no willingness to be friendly with me either. He was quite bright and he read very well, but he remained a long, watchful distance from me.

On my way home that evening I passed by a tiny hole-in-the-wall tobacconist's a short distance from the school. Hanging on the upper part of the open doorway was a black noticeboard on which were pinned a number of cards advertising goods for sale and accommodation required or available. I stopped for a moment and looked at the board. The long trip to Brentwood twice each day would be tiring enough during these fine May days; come winter with its wet and snow it would be worse. It might be a good idea to find suitable accommodation nearer the school.

'. . . help you?'

The man stood just inside the doorway of the shop, half camouflaged against the background of candy jars and slatted wooden boxes of soft drinks, his round unshaven face a pale blob above the collarless striped shirt which bulged heavily at the waist.

'Not really, I was just taking a look. I might like to find a room near by.'

He moved farther into the doorway, his thumbs hooked into the narrow braces from which his baggy trousers depended.

'Yes. Work around here?'

'I'm a teacher at Greenslade School – began today in fact.'

At this he screwed up his eyes as if the better to focus them on me; his look was careful, comprehensive.

'Teacher, ah yes.' He moved closer to me and pointed a stubby forefinger at the noticeboard without relinquishing his thumbgrip on the braces, so that it made an angular bow with his body.

'These not good for you; for teacher not good. Sometimes good ones I have, these not.'

I looked at him in some surprise; this was quite unexpected.

'Other times you come, something good I tell.'

He smiled and turned back into his shop, and I walked on in wonderment at the amazing unexpectedness of human kindness.

At home that evening I discussed the situation in the classroom with Mom and Dad Belmont and listened carefully to their counsel. We agreed that it was very necessary for me to gain the children's confidence and respect before their resentment crystallised into some unpleasant incident which might for ever wreck any possibility of future good relationship with them.

CHAPTER 8

EACH FRIDAY MORNING the whole school spent the pre-recess period in writing their Weekly Review. This was one of the Old Man's pet schemes; and one about which he would brook no interference. Each child would review the events of his school week in his own words, in his own way; he was free to comment, to criticise, to agree or disagree, with any person, subject or method, as long as it was in some way associated with the school. No one and nothing was sacred, from the Headmaster down, and the child, moreover, was safe from any form of reprisal.

'Look at it this way,' Mr Florian had said. 'It is of advantage to both pupil and teacher. If a child wants to write about something which matters to him, he will take some pains to set it down as carefully and with as much detail as possible; that must in some way improve his written English in terms of spelling, construction and style. Week by week we are able, through his reviews, to follow and observe his progress in such things. As for the teachers, we soon get a pretty good idea what the children think of us and whether or not we are getting close to them. It may sometimes be rather deflating to discover that a well-prepared lesson did not really excite Johnny Smith's interest, but, after all, the lesson was intended to benefit Johnny Smith, not his teacher; if it was uninteresting to him then the teacher must think again. You will discover that these children are reasonably fair, even when they comment on us. If we are careless about our clothing, manners or person they will soon notice it, and it would be pointless to be angry with them for pointing such things out. Finally, from the reviews, the sensible teacher will observe the trend of individual and collective interests and plan his work accordingly.'

On the first Friday of my association with the class I was anxious to discover what sort of figure I cut in front of them, and what kind of comment they would make about me. I read through some of the reviews at lunchtime, and must admit to a mixture of relief and disappointment at discovering that, apart from mentioning that they had a new 'blackie' teacher, very little attention was given to me. They were more concerned with the sudden failure of the radiogram during their dance session the previous Wednesday, and the success some of the boys had had as representatives of the local club's boxing team.

It occurred to me that they probably imagined I would be as transient as my many predecessors, and therefore saw no point in wasting either time or effort in writing about me. But if I had made so little impression on them, it must be my own fault, I decided. It was up to me to find some way to get through to them.

Thereafter I tried very hard to be a successful teacher with my class, but somehow, as day followed day in painful procession, I realised that I was not making the grade. I bought and read books on the psychology of teaching in an effort to discover some way of providing the children with the sort of intellectual challenge to which they would respond, but the suggested methods somehow did not meet my particular need, and just did not work. It was as if I were trying to reach the children through a thick pane of glass, so remote and uninterested they seemed.

Looking back, I realise that in fact I passed through three phases in my relationship with them. The first was the silent treatment, and during that time, for my first few weeks, they would do any task I set them without question or protest, but equally without interest or enthusiasm; and if their interest was not required on the task in front of them they would sit and stare at me with the same careful, patient attention a birdwatcher devotes to the rare feathered visitor. I would sit at my desk busily correcting some of their written work and feel their eyes on me, then look up to see them sitting there, watchful, waiting. It made me nervous and irritable, but I kept a grip on myself.

I took great pains with the planning of my lessons, using illustrations from the familiar things of their own background. Arithmetic was related to the kinds of problems which would conceivably occupy them and their parents within the domestic scene; the amount of money coming into and going out of a household, for instance, and the relative weights of foods and fuels and the measurements of familiar journeys or materials. I created varying problems within the domestic framework, and tried to encourage their participation, but it was as though there was a conspiracy of disinterest, and my attempts at informality fell pitifully flat.

Gradually they moved on to the second and more annoying phase of their campaign, the 'noisy' treatment. It is true to say that all of them did not actively join in this, but those who did not were obviously in some sympathy with those who did. During a lesson, especially one in which it was necessary for me to read or speak to them, someone would lift the lid of a desk and then let it fall with a loud bang; the culprit would merely sit and look at me with wide innocent eyes as if it were an accident. They knew as well as I did that there was nothing I could do about it, and I bore it with as much show of aplomb as I could manage. One or two such interruptions during a lesson were usually enough to destroy its planned continuity, and I was often driven to the expedient of bringing the reading to an abrupt halt and substituting some form of written work; they could not write and bang their desks at the same time.

I knew I could not long continue this type of pointless substitution. It was very clear to me that most of my teaching would be by word of mouth method because of the rather low academic standard of the class in general; everything must be made fully explicit, and I could not possibly avoid doing a great deal of talking. So I felt angry and frustrated when they rudely interrupted that which was being done purely for their own benefit. I did my best to keep these difficulties from my colleagues. I was very keen to disprove the distaff view that the men teachers were inadequate for the job, and I had no wish to give Weston any occasion for gloating, so I kept plugging away, tailoring the lessons to suit the children. I would sometimes walk around the neighbourhood after school to learn something of the background in and against which they had been reared, and though this helped me to understand the absence of certain social niceties from their conduct, it made that conduct no more bearable.

One morning I was reading to them some simple poetry, trying, by careful exposition and analysis, to give them something of the beauty it contained both in form and imagery. Just when I thought I had inveigled them into active interest, one of the girls, Monica Page, let the top of her desk fall; the noise seemed to reverberate in every part of my being and I felt a sudden burning anger. I looked at her for some moments before daring to open my mouth; she returned my gaze, then casually remarked to the class at large: 'The bleeding thing won't stay up.' It was all rather deliberate, the noisy interruption and the crude remark, and it heralded the third or bawdy stage of their conduct. From then on the words 'bloody' or 'bleedin'' were hardly ever absent from any remark they made to one another, especially in the classroom. They would call out to each other on any silly pretext and refer to the 'bleedin'' this or that, and always in a voice loud enough for my ears. One day during an arithmetic period, Jane Purcell called out to me: 'Can't do this sum, Mr Braithwaite, it's too bleedin' hard,' and sat there looking coolly up at me, her large breasts greasily outlined beneath the thin jumper, her eyes innocently blue in appeal.

'Tell me,' I replied, my voice chill and cutting with repressed anger: 'Do you use such words when speaking to your father?'

'You're not my bleeding father.' Her voice was flat and vicious. I was answered, and I shut up. You nasty little slut, I thought, I played right into your hand.

When the bell sounded for morning recess they rushed out into the corridor and I could hear her being congratulated for 'putting the black bastard in his place'. Some of her familiars loudly protested against my question, considering it 'f—ing cheek' and expressed in clear Anglo-Saxon words what their replies would have been if I had dared to make any comment about their parents. Somehow or other my attempt to correct the girl's language had been translated into a vicious and unwarranted attack on her parents.

After this incident things became slightly worse than before, and I could not escape the feeling that Weston had every justification for his attitude to the children; their viciousness was so pointless, so very unnecessary. Apart from their language other things were disturbing me. I would often come upon them, boys and girls, in the corridors or on the gloomy stairways, kissing and fondling with adult intentness; at my appearance they would break off and stand about, merely waiting for me to move on so they could resume their interrupted pleasures. After school they would hang about on the stairs or in the washroom, the girls laughingly protesting against the boys' advances in noisy, bawdy terms; or sometimes I would see a group of them in a corner of the playground in a kind of combined operation.

Although I argued with myself that their conduct, especially outside the classroom, was no business of mine, I could not escape a growing concern about them and about my relationship with them. Besides, the younger children were imitating the behaviour of the older ones, and some of the more adventurous small boys would even make 'passes' at the older girls. One small boy miraculously escaped serious injury when he crashed through the glass roof of the girls' lavatory while trying to spy on them.

This incident caused some very heated discussion in the staffroom, but oddly enough it was more concerned with the difficulties which would have resulted if he had seriously injured himself, than with the essential moral questions involved. The girls, too, rapidly recovered from the shock of being suddenly showered with broken glass and could be heard with their cronies in the corridor outside the classroom, laughingly reproving the absent adventurer for his stupidly roundabout way to so unimportant a discovery.

Matters came to a head one afternoon during recess. I had gone to the staffroom to fetch a cup of tea and returned to find the classroom smoky from an object which was smouldering in the grate of the fireplace. Several girls and boys were standing around joking and laughing, careless of the smoke and making no attempt to smother or remove its source. I pushed through them for a closer look, and was horrified to see that someone had thrown a used sanitary napkin into the grate and made an abortive attempt to burn it.

I was so overcome by anger and disgust that I completely lost my temper. I ordered the boys out of the room, then turned the full lash of my angry tongue on those girls. I told them how sickened I was by their general conduct, crude language, sluttish behaviour, and of their free and easy familiarity with the boys. The words gushed out of me, and the girls stood there and took it. By God, they took it! Not one of them dared to move or speak. Then I turned to their latest escapade.

'There are certain things which decent women keep private at all times, and I would have thought that your mother or older sisters would have explained such things to you, but evidently they have failed in that very obvious duty Only a filthy slut would have dared to do this thing, and those of you who stood by and encouraged her are just as bad. I do not wish to know which individual is responsible, because you are all to blame. I shall leave the classroom for exactly five minutes, in which time I expect that disgusting object to be removed and the windows opened to clear away the stink. And remember, all of you, if you must play these dirty games, play them in your homes, but not in my classroom.' With that I stormed out of the room, banging the door behind me.

I went upstairs and sat in the library, the only place where I could be alone for a little while. I felt sick at heart, because it seemed that this latest act, above all others, was intended to show their utter disrespect for me. They seemed to have no sense of decency, these children; everything they said or did was coloured by an ugly viciousness, as if their minds were forever rooting after filth. 'Why, oh why,' I asked myself, 'did they behave like that?' It was nothing to do with my being a Negro, I felt sure, because Hackman had not fared much better. Then what was it? What was wrong with them? They're trying to break me, I thought, they want to make me into another Hackman, lurking away in the staffroom when I should be in the classroom, should be the teacher in charge – the boss – as Clinty had said. That was it! They wanted to repeat their victory over Hackman. Fine, we'd see! I had done everything I could to meet them halfway, even more than halfway, but now I would take a very different line with them, even at the risk of contravening the Headmaster's carefully expressed views. I was now no longer angry, but determined to take firm action to set my class in order. From now on the classroom would be kept clean, in every way; I would not be asking it of them, but, demanding it. No more 'bloody' or 'bleeding' or anything else of that nature. And quiet, we'd have that too. No more banging desks. They had pushed me about as far as I was willing to go; from now on I would do a little pushing on my own account.

When I entered the classroom at the end of recess, the fireplace was washed clean, the windows were open, and the children were sitting quietly in their places. The girls seemed sheepish and refused to meet my glance, and I realised with something of a shock that they (at least most of them) were ashamed; the boys, on the other hand, were watching me expectantly, as if waiting for me to say or do something. I made no reference to the incident. As far as I was concerned the party was over; but I would need a little time to think up some effective way of bringing that fact home to them.

CHAPTER 9

NEXT MORNING I had an idea. It was nothing clear cut, merely speculative, but I considered it all the way to school. Then, after assembly, as soon as they were quiet I waded in. This might be a bit rough, I thought, but here goes.

'I am your teacher, and I think it right and proper that I should let you know something of my plans for this class.' I tried to pitch my voice into its most informally pleasant register. 'We're going to talk, you and I, but we'll be reasonable with each other. I would like you to listen to me without interrupting in any way, and when I'm through any one of you may say your piece without interruption from me.' I was making it up as I went along and watching them; at the least sign that it wouldn't work I'd drop it, fast.

They were interested, in spite of themselves; even the husky, blasé Denham was leaning forward on his desk watching me.

'My business here is to teach you, and I shall do my best to make my teaching as interesting as possible. If at any time I say anything which you do not understand or with which you do not agree, I would be pleased if you would let me know. Most of you will be leaving school within six months or so; that means that in a short while you will be embarked on the very adult business of earning a living. Bearing that in mind, I have decided that from now on you will be treated, not as children, but as young men and women, by me and by each other. When we move out of the state of childhood certain higher standards of conduct are expected of us . . .'

At this moment the door was flung open and Pamela Dare

rushed in, somewhat breathlessly, to take her seat. She was very late.

'For instance,' I continued, 'there are really two ways in which a person may enter a room; one is in a controlled, dignified manner, the other is as if someone had just planted a heavy foot in your backside. Miss Dare has just shown us the second way; I'm quite sure she will now give us a demonstration of the first.'

To this day I do not know what made me say it, but there it was. I was annoyed with the way in which she had just barged her way in, insolently carelessly late.

All eyes were on her as she had probably planned, but instead of supporting her entrance they were watching her, waiting to see the result of my challenge. She blushed.

'Well, Miss Dare?'

Her eyes were black with anger and humiliation, but she stood up and walked out, closing the door quietly behind her; then to my surprise, and I must confess, my relief, she opened it as quietly, and with a grace and dignity that would have befitted a queen, she walked to her seat.

'Thank you. As from today there are certain courtesies which will be observed at all times in this classroom. Myself you will address as "Mr Braithwaite" or "Sir" – the choice is yours; the young ladies will be addressed as "Miss" and the young men will be addressed by their surnames.'

I hadn't planned any of this, but it was unfolding all by itself, and, I hoped, fitting into place. There was a general gasp at this, from boys and girls alike.

Potter was the first to protest.

'Why should we call 'em "Miss", we know 'em.'

'What is your name?'

'Potter.'

'I beg your pardon?'

'Potter, Sir.' The 'Sir' was somewhat delayed.

'Thank you, Potter. Now, is there any young lady present whom you consider unworthy of your courtesies?'

'Sir?'

'Is there any one of these young ladies, who you think does not deserve to be addressed as Miss?'

With one accord the girls turned to look at Potter, as if daring him; he quailed visibly before their concerted eyes and said, 'No, Sir.'

'You should remember, Potter, that in a little while all of you may be expected to express these courtesies as part of your jobs; it would be helpful to you to become accustomed to giving and receiving them.'

I walked around my desk and sat in my chair. For the time being at least they were listening, really listening to me; maybe they would not understand every word, but they'd get the general import of my remarks.

'The next point concerns the general deportment and conduct of the class. First, the young ladies. They must understand that in future they must show themselves both worthy and appreciative of the courtesies we men will show them. As Potter said, we know you. We shall want to feel proud to know you, and just how proud we shall feel will depend entirely on you. There are certain things which need attention, and I have asked Mrs Dale-Evans to discuss them with you in your Domestic Science period today.' This last bit was right off the cuff; I'd have to see Grace about it during recess, but I felt sure she'd help.

'Now the boys. I have seen stevedores and longshoremen who looked a lot cleaner and tidier. There is nothing weak and unmanly about clean hands and faces and shoes that are brushed. A man who is strong and tough never needs to show it in his dress or the way he cuts his hair. Toughness is a quality of the mind, like bravery or honesty or ambition; it has nothing whatever to do with muscles. I suppose that in about a year or so some of you will be thinking of girlfriends; believe me, they will think you much more attractive with clean teeth, hands and faces than without.'

I gave them a moment to digest that.

'You are the top class; the operative word is "top". That means you must set the standard in all things for the rest of the school, for, whether you wish it or no, the younger ones will ape everything you do or say. They will try to walk like you and use the words you use, and dress like you, and so, for as long as you're here, much of their conduct will be your responsibility. As the top class you must be top in cleanliness, deportment, courtesy and work. I shall help you in every way I can, both by example and encouragement. I believe that you have it in you to be a fine class, the best this school has ever known, but I could be wrong; it all depends on you. Now, any questions?'

A hand shot up.

'Yes, Miss Joseph?'

'What about Mr Weston, he's never tidy, and his shoes are never clean, Sir.'

Things were looking up already; the 'Sir' came easily.

'Mr Weston is a teacher. Miss Joseph, and we shall not discuss him.'

There was a murmur of dissent at this.

'I am your teacher, and I'm the one you should criticise if I fail to maintain the standards I demand of you.'

There was an absence of the silent hostility of yesterday. I felt that I had somehow won for myself a breathing space at least. There were no further questions, so I told them they could spend the remaining minutes of that period considering and discussing the things I had said, providing they did so quietly. I sat back and observed them.

At recess I went to the staffroom and told Grace how I had impulsively committed her to a talk with the girls; she was quite pleased about it and promised to 'lay it on thick'.

That day passed pleasantly enough. I felt more at ease with them and applied myself enthusiastically to each subject, blending informality with a correctness of expression which I hoped would in turn help them to improve their own speech. I never spoke down to them; if they did not quite understand every word I used, the meaning was sufficiently clear in context, and I encouraged them to ask for an explanation any time they felt unsure. Meanwhile I was careful to discover the centres of leadership among them. Denham had quite a following among the boys; Potter, big and beefy, seemed to tag along with Denham through sheer laziness in asserting himself; Fernman and Seales were somewhat solitary characters, although they worked extremely well in class and played as boisterously in the playground as anyone else. I had expected that Pamela Dare would be a leader among the girls, but this did not prove to be so; she had one or two familiars, but kept very much to herself with a certain sullenness which I found both strange and intriguing. She was easily the brightest pupil, and her written work was neat and precise, in keeping with her personal appearance. Moira Joseph was the girl around whom the others circulated. She was tall, slim and vivacious, with a certain natural inclination to and aptitude for innocent seductiveness; most of the boys were ready to eat out of her hand. If I could get these king-pins to co-operate the others would probably fall in line.

On my way home that evening I walked to the bus with Miss Blanchard, and told her about what I had done. She was dubious about the wisdom of imposing unfamiliar social codes on the children, yet, as I had already committed myself, she hoped it would work. I was secretly pleased at the concern in her large eyes and felt more than ever determined to make a success of the class.

CHAPTER 10

IT WAS FRIDAY morning and I sat at my desk watching the absorbed application of the class as they wrote up their Weekly Review. They were very quiet, and I wondered what sort of reviews would result from the very recent happenings in the classroom. Soon after they began writing Jackson asked: 'How do you spell your name, Sir?' For his edification and that of any other I wrote my name in block capitals on the blackboard, and thereafter the only sounds were the rustle of turned pages or the occasional clatter of a dropped pencil.

I read through some of the reviews at lunchtime. They were, as Mr Florian had said, reasonably fair, but only just so. Without exception they commented on the new method of addressing each other, but avoided any reference to the events leading up to those measures. Some of the boys thought it was silly to have to 'call the tarts in the class "Miss",' and pointed out that once outside the school 'they'd get called some right names'. Some girls thought it sheer cheek on my part to have Mrs Dale-Evans talk to them about washing themselves and their clothing; they were sure they were clean because they bathed every Friday night. Nonetheless, one thing clearly emerged: they were very pleased to be treated like grown-ups, to be talked to like equals. Fernman wrote: 'He speaks to us as if we understand all the words he uses, and most of us try to look as if we do.' I smiled at this; they were already showing their stuff.

I took the reviews home that evening. I wanted to hear the comments of Mom and Dad. After dinner we sat around and talked about it; they were very pleased with the way things were moving, but advised caution. Then Dad said:

'Don't fall into the habit of bringing work home, Rick. It indicates a lack of planning, and you would eventually find yourself stuck indoors every night. Teaching is like having a bank account. You can happily draw on it while it is well supplied with new funds; otherwise you're in difficulties.

'Every teacher should have a fund of ready information on which to draw; he should keep that fund supplied regularly by new experiences, new thoughts and discoveries, by reading and moving around among people from whom he can acquire such things.'

'Not much chance of social movement for me, I'm afraid.'

'Nonsense, Rick, you're settled in a job now, so there's no need to worry about that; but you must get out and meet more people. I'm sure you'll find lots of nice people about who are not foolishly concerned with prejudice.'

'That's all right, Dad; I'm quite happy to stay at home with you and Mom.'

'Nice to hear you say that, but we're old and getting a bit stuffy. You need the company of younger people like yourself. It's even time he had a girl, don't you think, Jess?'

Mom smiled across at me.

'Ah, leave him alone, Bob, there's plenty of time for that.'

We went on to chat about other things, but I never forgot what Dad Belmont had said, and never again did I take notebooks home for marking. I would check the work in progress by moving about the class, helping here, correcting there; and I very soon discovered that in this way errors were pin-pointed while they were still fresh in the child's mind.

As the days followed each other my relationship with the children improved. At first there was much shamefaced resistance to addressing the girls as 'Miss', but gradually they settled down to it and the results were very encouraging. They also began to take greater care with their appearance, and their conduct was generally less boisterous.

I talked to them about everything and anything, and frequently the bell for recess, dinner or the end of the day would find us deep in interested discussion. I sought to relate each lesson to themselves, showing them that the whole purpose of their education was the development of their own thinking and reasoning. Some of them proved to be very intelligent – Pamela Dare, Potter, Tich Jackson, Larry Seales, Fernman – while others exhibited a native intelligence somewhat removed from academic pursuits, yet vitally necessary in the unrelenting struggle for survival with which they were already familiar. They asked me about myself – place of birth, education, war service – with an interest which was forthright and friendly.

Not all of them. Denham and a few of his intimates remained watchfully hostile, losing no opportunity to 'take the Mickey out of me'; they were discreetly disrespectful and persisted in their scruffy appearance as a sign of their resistance to my authority. They were few in number, and I planned to take as little notice as possible of their attitude, in the fond hope that it would disappear under pressure of the predominant co-operation.

But it was not to be as easy as that. One morning our Geography lesson dealt with clothing: we discussed the type and amount of garments worn by people in varying climatic conditions – Eskimos of the Frigid Zone and their dress of skins; the thin cotton garments worn by Caribbean folk of the semi-torrid climes.

'Sir, I have a magazine at home, Sir, all with women with no clothes on at the top, black women, Sir, dancing and that.' Tich Jackson's piping voice carried a hint that his interest in the magazine was not entirely academic.

'Yes, Jackson, many people in the tropics wear very little clothing; some primitive folk are even quite content with a daub of paint here and there.'

'Like the ancient Britons, Sir, they painted themselves.'

'Yes, Miss Dare, but we must remember that painting was intended merely as decoration, and not as a means of protection from climatic conditions. Some people paint themselves in startling ways so as to strike fear into the hearts of their enemies. Some African and North American Indian tribes were very much inclined to do that.'

'They must have been cold, Sir.'

'Who, Miss Benjamin?'

'What you said, Sir, the ancient Britons and that.'

'Not really; they lived in caves and dressed themselves in the skins of animals.'

'Fancy seeing a cave woman in a fur coat!'

Denham was always in there, sharp, quick, never missing a chance. The class laughed at his sally and I joined in; the image was really funny.

'Not cut to present day style, Denham, but utilitarian.'

He'd shut up while he worked that one out.

'Since the days when the ancient Britons collected their fur coats straight from the animals, clothing in Britain has passed through several important stages and changes; there is at the moment an exhibition at the Victoria and Albert Museum which illustrates this change. If any of you are interested, I would suggest that you go and see it when you can.'

'Why don't you take us, Sir?'

Barbara Pegg was the large, freckled girl whose eyes always held a smile. She was looking at me hopefully. I had never thought of doing anything like that, taking this crowd round and about London, yet I found myself replying:

'If enough of you are interested, Miss Pegg, I'll discuss it with Mr Florian.'

'Oh, yes, Sir,' many of them quickly agreed.

There was the sound of tittering from the back row, and glancing towards it I noticed that Denham and Sapiano, one of his cronies, were amusing themselves with something which Denham had in his half-open desk. I walked over and pulled the lid of the desk fully open; inside was a copy of *Weekend Mail* which featured an enlarged picture of a well-favoured young woman in the briefest of bikinis; Denham was busy with his pencil in a way which defeated the already limited purpose of the scanty costume.

I picked up the paper and closed the desk. Denham leaned back in his chair and smiled at me insolently – he had wanted me to find it. Without a word I tore the disgusting thing to shreds, walked back to my desk and dumped them into the waste-basket. As I turned away from him I distinctly heard the muttered 'F—ing black bastard.' I continued with the lesson as if nothing had happened.

Denham's face was now a picture of vicious anger. He had wanted a row, that he might in some way upset the class, and he felt checked. The others looked at me in alarm when I tore up the paper – they were familiar with Denham's reputation, and their surprised, anxious faces warned me that something unpleasant was in store.

I was soon to find out what it was.

CHAPTER 11

ON THURSDAY MORNING the class seemed to be in the grip of some excitement and expectancy. During recess they stood about the classroom in little whispering groups which fell silent as I approached, but I could read no special significance into this. The lessons proceeded more or less normally, but heavily.

In the afternoon, we went down to the gym for the usual P.T. period. The equipment was neatly arranged around the cleared dining hall; vaulting horse, buck, jumping standards, medicine balls, boards, several pairs of boxing gloves slung by their laces across the vaulting horse. The boys were, with one exception, barefoot and wearing only blue shorts. Sapiano sat on a low form, his right arm bandaged from elbow to wrist.

'Line up in the centre, will you,' I began.

They eagerly obeyed, forming two neatly graded lines. But then Denham stepped forward.

'Please, Sir.'

'Yes, Denham?'

'Can't we have boxing first today, please, Sir?'

'Why, Denham?'

'Oh, nothing, Sir, just feel we'd like to have a bit of a change, Sir.'

'Oh, very well,' I replied. 'Get yourselves into pairs according to size.'

The pairing was completed in a moment as if by pre-arrangement; only Denham remained unpaired.

'My partner's crippled, Sir.' He indicated the bandaged Sapiano. 'Will you have a go with me?'

At this the others, as if on cue, moved quietly towards us, watchful, listening.

'You can wait and have a bout with Potter or one of the others.'

The pieces were falling into place, the penny had finally and fatefully dropped.

'They'll be done in, Sir, I don't mind having a knock with you.'

'Go on, Sir, take him on.'

This chorus of encouragement was definitely not in my best interest.

'No, Denham, I think you'll have to skip it for today.'

Denham looked at me pityingly, slipped the gloves off his large hands and casually dropped them at my feet. He had made his point. Looking quickly at the others I could read the disappointment and disgust in their faces. They thought I was afraid, scared of the hulking, loutish fellow.

'Okay, let's go.'

I took a pair of gloves from the horse. Potter stepped over and expertly secured the laces for me while Sapiano, strangely unhampered by his mysterious injury, did the same for Denham. The others meanwhile ranged themselves along the wall, silent and expectant.

As we began to box it became clear that Denham's reputation as a boxer was thoroughly justified; he was fast and scored easily, though his blows were not delivered with his full weight. I tried to dodge and parry as best I could, being only concerned with riding this out for a little while until I could reasonably stop it. I had stupidly allowed myself to be lured into this one, and it was up to me to extricate myself with as little damage to either dignity or person as I could.

'Come on, Sir, go after him.' I recognised Patrick Fernman's voice. Disappointment was poignant in it; they must all be somewhat surprised at my lame efforts.

Suddenly Denham moved in and hit me in the face; the blow stung me and I could feel my eyes filling up with tears;

the salt blood in my mouth signalled other damage. I was angry now, this was no longer a pleasant little affair – the fellow meant business. It may have been the sight of the blood on my face, or the insistent urging of his cronies to 'Go arter 'im'; whatever it was, it spelled Denham's undoing. Guard open, he rushed in and I hit him; my gloved fist sank deep into his solar-plexus, and the air sighed out of him as he doubled up and collapsed on the floor.

There was a moment of stunned silence, then Potter and some others rushed to help him.

'Hold it. Leave him where he is and line up quickly for vaulting. Clarke, collect the gloves and stack them by the door.'

To my amazement they obeyed without demur, while I hurried to Denham and helped him over to a low form against the wall; he was only winded and would soon be right as rain. When he was comfortable I continued with the P.T. lesson, which went without a hitch; the boys were eager to do their best, and went through the various movements without recourse to my prompting or direction; they now looked at me as if I had suddenly and satisfactorily grown up before their very eyes.

At the end of the lesson I dismissed class and went over to Denham; he still looked a bit green.

'That was just a lucky punch, old man; no harm meant. Why don't you pop up to the washroom and soak your head in some cold water? You'll feel a lot better.'

'Yes, Sir.' His voice was shaky, but there was no hesitation or mimicry about the 'Sir'. I helped him to his feet and he signalled to Potter, who went off with him towards the washroom.

That incident marked a turning point in my relationship with the class. Gradually Denham's attitude changed, and like it that of his cronies. He could still be depended on to make a wisecrack or comment whenever the opening presented itself, but now these were more acceptable to all of us, for they were no longer made in a spirit of rebellion and viciousness. He appeared clean and more and more helpful and courteous, and with this important area of resistance dispelled the class began to move into high gear. Moreover, I suddenly became aware of an important change in my own relationship to them. I was experiencing more than a mere satisfaction in receiving their attention, obedience and respect with their acceptance of my position as their teacher. I found myself liking them, really liking them, collectively and singly. At first I had approached each school day a little worried, a little frightened, but mostly determined to make good for the job's sake; now there had occurred in me a new attitude, a concern to teach them for their own sakes, and a deep pleasure at every sign that I had succeeded. It was a delight to be with them, and more and more I had occasion to wonder at their generally adult viewpoint. I was learning a little more of them each day. Some of them would remain in the classroom during recess and we'd talk about many things.

They were mostly from large families and understood the need and importance of money; they even felt that they should already be at work to help ease the financial strain on their parents, and to meet their own increasing demands for clothing, cosmetics, entertainment, etc. They spoke of overcrowding, marriage and children with casual familiarity; one girl had helped with the unexpected birth of her baby brother and spoke of it with matronly concern.

The lessons were taking hold. I tried to relate everything academic to familiar things in their daily lives. Weights were related to foodstuffs and fuel, measurements to dress-lengths, linoleum and carpets; in this way they could see the point of it all, and were more prepared to pursue the more abstract concepts. In Geography and History we talked and read, and here I was in the very fortunate position of being able to illustrate from personal experiences. They eagerly participated, asking me questions with a keenness I had not suspected in them, and often the bell for recess, lunch or the end of the day would find us in the heat of some discussion, disinclined to leave off.

The Headmaster would occasionally drop in unexpectedly, and would sometimes find himself drawn into discussions on some point or other; he was pleased, and expressed his satisfaction with my efforts. On one such occasion I mentioned the idea of the visit to the Victoria and Albert Museum.

'I wouldn't advise it,' he replied. 'You have settled in very nicely with them here, but taking them across London would be another matter entirely.'

'I think they'll be okay, Sir.'

'There's always a tendency for the best of children to show off when out of the closed supervision of the school confines, and these are no exception, they're probably worse than most. After all, you cannot hope to supervise forty-six children by yourself.'

'I'd like to try, Sir.'

'Out of the question, Braithwaite, but I'll say this. If you can persuade another teacher to go with you, you may. It's entirely against the Council's rules for one teacher to have charge of so many children outside the school.'

'I'll see if I can get someone to go with me.'

'Fine, if she's agreeable let me know and I'll arrange for a travel warrant.'

He was smiling slyly and I wondered who it was he had in mind.

'But what about that teacher's own class, Sir?'

'Don't worry. I'll supervise it for the occasion.'

At lunch I mentioned the plan to Miss Blanchard.

'Would you like to help me with them, Miss Blanchard?'

'Gillian.'

'Ricky.' She smiled. 'Well, will you?'

'I'd love to. When do you plan to go?'

'As soon as the Head can arrange for the travel warrant.'

This was fine.

'Why didn't you ask Miss Clintridge?'

'Just didn't think of it, I suppose.'

'Oh.' There was playful mockery in those eyes.

When the rest of the staff returned from the dining hall I mentioned the idea of the trip, and that Miss Blanchard had agreed to accompany me. They were, to say the least, very dubious about it. While I sat there listening to them there was a knock on the door. Weston opened it to Patrick Fernman, who asked:

'Please, Sir. Miss Dare would like to know if anyone has fixed the girls' netball.'

'Miss Who?' Weston's voice was shrill with astonishment.

'Miss Dare, Sir.' Fernman looked at the puzzled face and supplied: 'Pamela Dare, Sir.'

Without replying Weston walked away from the door to lean against the fireplace, his face a study in exaggerated amazement. I meanwhile took a netball from the sports cupboard and gave it to Fernman, who quickly disappeared, noisily slamming the door in his haste.

'Well, I'll be damned.' Weston was smiling, but there was a sneer near the surface of his smile. 'Fancy that. "Miss Dare would like the netball." ' He pointed his pipe at me with a theatrical gesture. 'I say, whatever's going on in that classroom of yours, old man? I mean this suburban formality and all. Bit foreign in this neck of the woods, don't you think?'

'Is it really?' I enquired. It had not occurred to me that I would need to defend any improvement in the children's conduct or deportment, and I was not quite sure what Weston was getting at.

'What's it all in aid of, old man?' he continued; his hairy arm stuck out from the seedy, leather-trimmed sleeves like that of a scarecrow; the Wurzel Gummidge of the staffroom. 'Some sort of experiment in culture for the millions?'

'Not quite that,' I replied. 'Just an exercise in elementary courtesy. Does it bother you?' I was becoming a bit irritated by the smile and the unnatural patronising good humour.

'Bother me? Not at all old man. But tell me, do you also address them as "Miss", or are you exempt because of your, ah, privileged position?'

The rest of the staff were watching us and I felt very uncomfortable.

'I too address the girls as "Miss".'

'Thoroughly democratic and commendable,' he replied, the

forced smile becoming even sweeter. 'But tell me, are the rest of us uncouth critters expected to follow suit?'

'Not necessarily; it's merely that my class and I have reached an agreement on certain courtesies.'

'Thank God for that! I don't somehow see myself addressing those snotty little tarts as "Miss" along with Denham and Co.'

'Is it that you object to being taught a lesson in courtesy by those boys, Mr Weston?'

I could hardly believe my ears. That was Miss Dawes; I would never have thought of her as coming to anybody's defence, unless it was Miss Phillips'.

'I do not need lessons in manners from those morons – nor from professional virgins either, for that matter.'

Miss Dawes blushed, but continued bravely:

'As long as you learn, it doesn't matter who teaches, does it?'

'Good for you Josy,' Clinty interjected.

'Ah, well,' Weston resumed, 'I suppose it comes natural to some people to say: "Yes, Ma'am; yes Boss".'

His caricature of a subservient negro was so grotesque that I could almost smile. But the intention behind the words was not funny, and I was rather relieved when Grace, with her usual tact, broke into the conversation.

'By the way, Ricky,' she called to me, 'what have you been saying to Droopy?'

'Droopy? Who or what is Droopy?'

'Oh, come off it. I'm talking about Jane Purcell in your class. You know . . .' and she quoted: 'Uncorseted, her friendly bust gives promise, etc., etc.'

'Oh, I see. I haven't been saying anything to her specially. Why?'

'All of a sudden she's become very conscious of her, er, mammary glands.' Grace's laughter ran round the room until it found reflection in each face there.

'Now she wants advice on the right type of brassière – I never liked that word, it always sounds like a receptacle for hot coals.'

'Could be.' Clinty would never be outdone.

'Looks like she chose the right person to advise her.' Weston's owlish eyes were on Grace's attractive bust; I was sure the untidy fringe around his mouth hid the leer which his voice so clearly revealed.

'A little good advice wouldn't be wasted on you either, my lad.'

Grace's voice was very frosty now, and Weston shut up.

I felt slightly disturbed by the tensions generated within the staffroom. I had thought that my presence was the red rag to Weston's bull, but now I discovered that his attitude to me was only part of a general situation which had existed for some time before my arrival. Most of the women teachers were obviously fed up at being saddled with a male colleague who never joined in any conversation except to be sarcastic or critical. Gillian, I noticed, remained cool and untroubled by it. She seemed to be able to play the part of observer, letting any discord pass over her, confident in the assurance of her own poise and breeding to keep her inviolate. Miss Phillips seemed unaffected by it for different reasons; she spent her staffroom leisure in some strange world of fancy which was irrevocably closed to all except Miss Dawes, who also, until today's brave gesture, had never allowed anything which transpired to invade their tight, secret conclave.

But the clash of personalities in the staffroom was, after all, of no great importance, so long as its repercussions did not enter the classrooms. It was the children, not the teachers, who mattered.

CHAPTER 12

AFTER LUNCH THE class received the news of the trip to the Victoria and Albert Museum with delight. I told them it was planned for the following Thursday, and that Miss Blanchard would be coming along to help keep order. At this there was some good-natured twittering, and Pamela Dare asked:

'Does she have to come, Sir?'

'Oh yes, Miss Dare. The Council wouldn't allow forty-odd children to go on an expedition in the care of only one teacher.'

'I like Miss Blanchard, she's smashing.' Tich Jackson's puckish face creased in a smile of delight.

'Oh, shut up Tich, who asked you?' Tich looked at Pamela Dare in surprise; her tone was unnecessarily hostile.

'Jackson,' he said softly, 'the name's Jackson.'

The girl made a face at him and tossed her red hair defiantly.

On Thursday morning when I arrived I went to the Headmaster's office to collect the travel voucher for our trip and reached my classroom some time after they were all seated and waiting. I was quite unprepared for what I saw – the children were scrubbed, combed and brushed and shining. The girls were beautifully turned out and there was more than a suggestion of lipstick in evidence; the boys were smartly dressed, and everyone was beaming happily at my delighted surprise.

One seat was empty. Tich Jackson's. I called the register merely as a formality, for by now I could quickly spot an absence, so much a part of me had the class become.

I collected their dinner money and was waiting for Miss Blanchard when there was a slight commotion outside the door: I went across and pulled it open. On the threshold was a huge laundry bundle; and from somewhere underneath it a voice was crying:

'It's me, Sir, Jackson. Gotta take the bagwash for me Mum. Don't go without me, Sir, I'll be back in a jiff.' Without pausing for any reply the bundle was withdrawn and disappeared down the passage to a chorus of laughter from the class in which I joined helplessly.

Gillian soon arrived and we divided the class into two groups for easier control; and when Jackson returned we set off for the Underground Station.

At Whitechapel we changed to a District Line for South Kensington. At that time of morning there were not many seats available, and the children were strung out among two carriages in groups of three or four. I was sandwiched near a door with Moira Joseph, Barbara Pegg and Pamela Dare, who were chattering excitedly to me about the things we were likely to see. They were especially anxious to look at some very fine complicated hand-stitching about which Gillian had told them, and it pleased me to be so closely identified with their lively enthusiasm. At Cannon Street two elderly, well-dressed women joined the train, and stood in the crowd close to us. The stare of disapproval they cast in our direction was made very obvious; and soon they were muttering darkly something about 'shameless young girls and these black men'.

I felt annoyed and embarrassed, and hoped the girls were too absorbed in discussion to notice the remarks, which were meant to be overheard.

Barbara Pegg, who was closer to them than the others, was the first to hear them. She bent forward and whispered to Pamela, who moved around until she had changed places with Barbara and was next to the women. Suddenly she turned to face them, her eyes blazing with anger.

'He is our teacher. Do you mind?'

She had intended her voice to carry, and it did. The women looked away, shocked and utterly discomfited, as other people on the train turned to stare at the defiantly regal girl and the blushing busybodies who probably wished that they could sink through the floor.

At the museum the children were collected together for a final briefing. Equipped with paper and pencils they would work in groups of six or seven, each group concerning itself with some particular aspect of Mid-Victorian dress – design, material, stitch-craft, accessories, hair culture, wigs, etc. We would all meet in the museum canteen at eleven o'clock for a cup of tea, and again at twelve preparatory to returning to school. They were reminded to be very quiet and to refrain from touching any of the exhibits.

Gillian and I moved about among the little groups, giving advice and assistance. She was graceful and charming and made quite a hit with the boys who vied with each other for her attention.

It was for me a pleasant and revealing experience; I had not supposed that the children would have shown so much interest in historical events. Weston had even hinted that their enthusiasm for this outing was just one more excuse to get away from anything concerned with education; yet here they were, keenly interested, asking the sort of questions which clearly showed that they had done some preparatory work. They took the whole thing quite seriously, sketching, making notes, discussing it in undertones.

Later, I sat down to a cup of tea with Gillian, Patrick Fernman, Pamela and Barbara. It would have been difficult for a stranger to have guessed which of the three girls was the teacher, for Gillian was much smaller than the other two, who also looked more grown up than usual with the extra touch of red on their lips. Pamela especially was very striking, in a pleated red skirt set off by high-heeled red shoes and a saucy red ribbon worn high on her auburn hair. Looking at her I could see that in a few years she would really blossom out into something rather splendid.

'. . . it must have been very uncomfortable.'

I only caught the tail-end of Gillian's remark and looked at her guiltily.

'All the same, they must have looked smashing. Think of all that material for only one dress!' Barbara's large face was alive with enthusiasm.

The conversation centred around the exhibits they had seen; it was all very much outside their previous experience and interest, yet their comments were surprisingly shrewd. Fernman, whose parents worked in the clothing industry, showed an unexpected knowledge of the art of the Flemish weavers, and told us that his grandmother still wove in silk on her own hand loom.

I was thoroughly pleased with the conduct of my class; they would have been a credit to the best of schools. Denham and Potter had apparently elected themselves lieutenants, and just before twelve o'clock I could see them going from group to group marshalling the class together, and at a sign from me they led off through the subway towards the station.

Once on the train and released at last from the unusual strain of more than two hours of quiet, they were themselves again, joking and chattering about the things they had seen like a band of cheerful monkeys. Every now and then I could overhear the now familiar 'Sir said . . .' expressed with positive finality, a constant reminder of the great responsibility I had undertaken. They now accepted the things I said completely, unquestioningly, because they had accepted me, and no one seemed disposed to query the authenticity of anything which bore the seal 'Sir said'.

Back at school the children scattered towards the dining hall or home and Gillian and I went off to the staffroom. I had seen very little of her on the way back, and now as we settled down to our sandwiches she told me how much she had enjoyed the visit.

'It was so much nicer than I expected, Rick, I mean being with them off the school premises.'

'I know what you mean. They're really nice people, as Mrs Drew says.'

'It's more than that. On the way back I was talking with Moira Joseph and Effie Cook; they spoke to me as equals, and I had the odd feeling that they knew more about life than I did.'

'That's not surprising. Moira's mother has been in a convalescent home for nine weeks, tuberculosis I think, and Moira has to mother the family. Two younger ones are at a Junior School near by; she's allowed to leave school early each afternoon to collect them.'

'God, how dreadful!'

'I don't think she minds in the least; rather enjoys it, I suppose. She told me about the way her father praises her cooking. I do think we often make the mistake of lumping them all together as "kids".'

'Oh, I wouldn't call them that, not all of them anyway. The Dare girl has quite a crush on you, I've noticed.'

I sat looking at her, completely lost for words; women say the damnedest things.

'Well, you have noticed it, haven't you?' The smile did not detract from the serious note in her voice.

'No, I haven't. I treat her no differently from any of the others.'

'Now don't be silly, Rick. I'm sure you don't but that would make no difference. It's quite the usual thing, you know; I'm sure some of the small boys in my class are dying for love of me.' Her silvery laughter rang through the room; and I found it impossible to be annoyed with her.

'I hear you had a spot of bother on the train this morning.'

'Oh, nothing serious.' I described the incident and the way in which Pamela had effectively put the busybodies to rout. She gave me a long searching look.

'Rick, I think you're the one who's treating them like kids. But don't make that mistake with the Dare girl; she's a woman in every sense of the word.'

'Now, wait a moment, Gillian; there's nothing significant in Pamela's action in the train, at least, not to me.'

'Have it your own way. Not that I really blame the girl a bit – you are rather overpowering, you know.'

Immediately I felt a change in the atmosphere. Out of nowhere something had entered into our relationship, a new element which at once excited, delighted and sobered me. I suddenly felt agitated and confused; and, making some hasty and rather silly excuses, I left her and went down to my classroom to sort myself out. This thing had somehow caught me by surprise. Yet, as I sat there, I wondered whether I was being foolishly premature, reading too much into a simple remark. I liked Gillian immensely; there had sprung up between us a very delightful camaraderie which I cherished and wished above all else to preserve.

My life in England had not by any means been ascetic. During my student days I had had one or two affairs, temporary contacts which were fully appreciated as such on both sides; and under the tensions of operational flying and the uncertainty of survival, sex became merely part of the general scheme of things and I was no exception. Like many of the others I had dates; the colour of my skin was not important. As a matter of fact it helped, along with the fact that I was rather good at games – rugger, soccer, tennis, cricket, athletics. Together these things operated very much in my favour and the women were accommodating. Some of my less fortunate white colleagues suggested, without rancour, that the women might have been merely curious to discover the truth about the many stories concerning the supposedly exceptional sexual equipment and prowess of the Negro. In actual fact I found a number of pleasant companions, and I sincerely hope I achieved no special notoriety as a boudoir athlete.

But all that belonged to the past. My life was now adjusted to new and different conditions, and I needed to tread carefully every step of the way. I had frequently observed the disapproval on the faces of English people at the sight of a white woman in a Negro's company, and if I had forgotten, this morning's incident would have been a reminder. Sitting with Gillian in the safe comfort of the staffroom was one thing; exposing her to those hard stares and vindictive faces was another. How long would our happy association survive the malignity of stares which were deliberately intended to make the woman feel unclean, as if she had abjectly degraded not merely herself but all womanhood? Only the strongest women could survive such treatment.

It seems as though there were some unwritten law in Britain which required any healthy, able-bodied Negro resident there to be either celibate by inclination, or else a master of the art of sublimation. And were he to seek solace from prostitutes or 'easy' women, he would promptly be labelled as filthy and undesirable. Utterly, inhumanly unreasonable! We were to be men, but without manhood.

My mind was full of these thoughts as Gillian walked into my classroom. Her usually gentle face was grave and set, I stood up as she approached my table.

'What's the matter, Rick?'

'Oh, nothing really. I wanted to think about something for a while.'

'Couldn't it have waited until later?' Her dark eyes were glowing wonderfully in a face made pale by agitation.

'I suppose so. It was rather stupid of me. I'm sorry.'

'Was it because of what I said?' Her lips were quivering slightly, and I wanted only to take her in my arms.

'Partly. It was something I suddenly realised while you were speaking.'

'Something about me, about us?'

'Yes, about us.'

'I felt it too, Rick.'

I stared at her, feeling helplessly out of my depth. Things were happening so quickly I could hardly keep pace with them.

'Are you angry with me, Rick?'

'Angry? How could I be?'

'That's good.' The smile was back on her face. I was always fascinated by that smile. It began with a faint twitching near the corners of her mouth, then flashed quickly, like a streak of lightning, to illuminate the depths of her eyes.

'See you after school.' And she was gone, leaving me confused, bewildered, but gloriously happy.

The following morning I was a bit late for school. Those damned trains were becoming more and more unpredictable; they always managed to get held up just outside a station, so that there was no alternative to waiting. The children were all in their places when I arrived, and as I stepped into the room they greeted me as with one voice:

'Good morning, Sir.'

I was so surprised I must have gaped at them for a moment before returning their greeting. This had never happened before. Usually I greeted them first just before registration and would receive a reply from those who felt like it. This was overwhelmingly different.

I recovered myself and walked towards my table, and there it was. In the centre of my table was a large vase in which was neatly arranged a bunch of flowers. Some were slightly bedraggled; all had evidently been collected from the tiny backyards and window boxes of their homes. For me this was the most wonderful bouquet in the world; it was an accolade bestowed collectively by them on me. I turned to look at their pleased, smiling faces and said, with a full heart:

'Thank you, all of you.'

CHAPTER 13

THE VISIT TO the Victoria and Albert featured largely in their reviews that week. They commented on it freely and thoughtfully, and even on their own conduct. When Mr Florian read the reviews he was delighted, and expressed his willingness to help with any other visits I might plan in the future.

I had now been with the class two months, and every day our lessons were becoming more and more interesting. I used every device I could think of to stimulate their interest in their school-work; there was so much for me to do with them, so much leeway to make up. Our lessons were very informal, each one a kind of discussion in which I gave them a lead and encouraged them to express their views against the general background of textbook information.

A human skeleton which had long hung unused in the Science Room was pressed into service for practical Physiology, and these lessons soon become very popular. They asked questions and I answered them fully; I treated them as young men and women and they responded admirably. When I said that the skeleton was that of a female they required proof; and my explanation of the angle and depth of the pelvic basin and the reasons for it naturally led to questions and answers on sex, marriage, pregnancy, childbirth. I, in turn, was amazed at the extent of their knowledge acquired at first hand. As members of large families living cheek by jowl in small rooms they had seen and heard enough to dispel, at an early age, any childish myths about reproduction.

Even the silent Seales now began to speak up in class, and it was soon clear to us all that he was as well-informed as anyone and full of natural good humour.

I began one Geography lesson by saying:

'Geography is the study of places, and the people, flora, fauna and mineral deposits to be found there.'

'What's that, Sir, flora and that?'

'Flora is a term used to describe all vegetable growths either on land or water, trees, weeds, waterplants, cultivated plants, etc. Fauna refers to all animal life, large or small. Today we shall consider some aspects of life on the African continent.'

'You don't come from Africa, do you, Sir?' Seales enquired, though I had answered this question many times before.

'No, Seales, I was born in British Guiana.'

'Where's that, Sir?'

'It's on the northern coast of South America, the only British Colony there. You can easily find it on the map between Suriname and Venezuela.'

'That's the same as Demerara, isn't it, Sir, where the sugar comes from?' Fernman's question was one which I had been asked even by teachers on the staff, who were in the main sadly uninformed about the Colonial territories, protectorates and dependencies.

They knew that Jamaica produced sugar, rum and bananas, that Nigeria produced cocoa, and that British Guiana had large natural resources; but these names, though as familiar as the products with which they were associated, were of places far away, and no one seemed really interested in knowing anything about the peoples who lived there or their struggles towards political and economic betterment.

The other teachers, also, used the word 'native' as a generic term for all coloured peoples, even those resident in Britain; and their idea of the Negro was largely conditioned by the familiar caricature in books and films – a shiftless and indolent character, living either in a primitive mud hut or in the more deplorable shanty town, and meeting all life's problems with a flashing smile, a sinuous dance, and drum-assisted song.

It was not entirely their fault. They had been taught with the same textbooks that these children were using now, and had fully digested the concept that coloured people were physically, mentally, socially and culturally inferior to themselves, though it was rather ill-mannered actually to say so.

The children would often support their own arguments with quotations from these school textbooks and from others of more recent vintage, when I had been giving them a somewhat different account of the conditions in some Colonial territories; and so powerful is the written word that it was hard for them to disagree with what they had read. If on occasions I used myself as an example, they had an answer to that, too.

'But, Sir, you're different.'

I explained to Fernman, with the help of an atlas, that Demerara was merely one of the three large territories of British Guiana, and that sugar was only one of the important products.

'Anyway, we are getting away from our subject, which is Africa. That continent is particularly interesting because of its diversity of peoples, religions, origins, cultures and climatic conditions. Colours differ from the black skins of the Negroes of the Niger basin, through the paler skins of the various Arab peoples to the white skins of the European settlers.'

'South Africans are white, aren't they, Sir?'

'A South African is a native of South Africa, irrespective of the colour of his skin.'

'But all natives are black, Sir.'

'No, Fernman. You're a native of London and so is Seales, but you are of different colours. I am a native of British Guiana, and there are thousands of British Guianese who are white-skinned and blonde, red-headed or brunette.'

Hard work, with so little support from the textbooks, yet it was satisfying work with these eager, friendly youngsters.

One evening on my way home I saw the old tobacconist standing at his door. As I approached he beckoned me into the little shop which was crowded with candy jars and soda pop bottles, wooden cases and display trays. Then, leaning over the narrow counter, he shouted something in Yiddish, and from behind a half-hidden door a voice answered and a very stout matriarch emerged.

'Mama, this is the new teacher at Greenslade School.'

He opened his arms with a gesture of a conjurer exhibiting a rabbit. I smiled and bowed to the old lady, who returned the smile with interest.

'What's your name?' he asked.

'Braithwaite,' I replied, 'Ricardo Braithwaite.'

'I'm Pinkus and this is Mama Pinkus.' The introduction was effected with a filial devotion which was good to see.

'How d'you do, Mama Pinkus.'

'I think I know some place for you.' He went to the little noticeboard and removed a small card on which was written a short advertisement of a room to let nearby. 'Mama think is good room, maybe all right for you.'

I received the card from him and thanked them both. I was really touched by their kindness in remembering me and my enquiry for a room.

I thought it best to call at the advertised address without delay, for I had been late a number of times lately, and though Mr Florian was very understanding about the train service, I felt that I ought to find 'digs' nearer the school. If I were lucky I would then tell Mom and Dad, who I was sure would understand; if I were not successful, well, no harm had been done.

The address was one of a terrace in a rather dingy street, but the pavement outside the front door was, like its neighbours, scrubbed white, and the brass door knocker and lace window curtains bore testimony to the occupant's attention to cleanliness. Some of these local folk were as houseproud as duchesses. I knocked and presently the door was opened by a large, red-faced smiling woman.

'Good evening. I'm here to enquire about the room.'

Immediately the smile was replaced by the expression of cold withdrawal I had come to know so well.

'Sorry, I'm not letting.'

'Mr Pinkus told me about it just a few moments ago,' I persisted.

'Sorry, I've changed me mind.' Her arms were folded across her stomach, and the set face and bulk of her added to the finality of her words.

'Who's it, Mum?' a girlish voice enquired from somewhere behind her.

'Some darky here asking about the room.' Her mouth spat out the words as if each one was intended to revile.

Embarrassed to the point of anger, I was turning away when there was a sudden movement behind her and a voice cried in consternation:

'Oh Gawd, Mum, it's Sir, it's me teacher.' Beside the woman's surprised face I caught a glimpse of the startled, freckled countenance of Barbara Pegg. 'Oh me Gawd. . . . '

I promised myself that that was my first and last attempt at finding other 'digs'. For as long as Mom and Dad would have me, theirs was my home. But for some time afterwards poor Barbara avoided me and blushed in confusion if I even spoke to her during lessons.

A few weeks later, I had my first date with Gillian. Since the day of our visit to the museum we had, by unspoken agreement, avoided the very personal things we both wanted to say, yet everything only served to underscore the strong affection we felt for each other, which increased in depth and intensity every day.

It was Gillian who finally proposed that we spend an evening together – and a wonderful evening it proved to be. We laughed and talked, held hands in the cinema, supped in Soho, and enjoyed every moment of each other's company. I had never been so happy.

Soon we were going regularly together to the theatre, ballet and films. On these occasions, Gillian told me more about herself. Her parents lived at Richmond: her father, often abroad, was in some way connected with international finance; her mother was a fashion designer. She herself had a flat in Chelsea, going home to Richmond whenever it was possible for them all to be together. Since leaving college two years ago, she had decided to be independent and earn her own living. She had worked for eighteen months in the Editorial Department of a woman's magazine but had tired of it and decided to try teaching; not so much for the money, as she had a very generous annual allowance to which both her parents contributed, but because teaching brought her in touch with people in a very personal way.

One afternoon, after the class was ended for the day, I was alone in my classroom correcting papers, when there was a knock and Mrs Pegg entered. I stood up and invited her to come in.

'Good afternoon, Mrs Pegg.'

'Good afternoon, Sir. I see you've remembered me.'

I did not reply to this, but waited for her to continue.

'I want to talk to you about the room, Sir. You see I didn't know that you was Babs' teacher, you know what I mean.'

I knew what she meant then, and I knew what she meant now.

'I think we'll just forget about the whole thing, Mrs Pegg.'

'But I can't forget about it, Sir. Babs has been after me day and night to come and talk to you about it. You can have the room if you like, Sir.'

'That's all right, Mrs Pegg. I've changed my mind about the room.'

'Have you got another one somewhere else locally, Sir?'

'No, Mrs Pegg, I've decided to remain where I am, at least for the present.'

'What shall I tell Babs, Sir? She'll think you're still mad at me, that's why you won't have the room.'

There was very real concern in her voice. Barbara must be quite a girl, I thought, to be able to put the fear of God into someone as massive and tough-looking as her mother.

'Leave it to me, Mrs Pegg. I will have a word with Barbara and explain the situation to her.'

'Oh, Sir, I'd be glad if you would; I didn't mean no harm that day, and she won't let me forget it.'

I was finally able to get rid of her. I did not believe for one moment that she cared whether I found a room or not, but, as was characteristic of so many of these women, she would have willingly submerged her own opinions and prejudices to please her daughter. I was not, on reflection, bitter about Mrs Pegg's refusal. It was understandable that in the present state of things a mother might be disinclined to have a male lodger sharing the same small house with her teenage daughter; my being a Negro might even strengthen that disinclination, though it could not excuse her crudely discourteous behaviour. What really mattered was that Barbara did not share her mother's snap prejudices; if the young ones were learning to think for themselves in such things, then even that painful incident had been worth something.

Later that day I found an opportunity to talk with Barbara. I mentioned that her mother had wanted me to take the room but that I had decided to stay where I was.

'But you would have had it at first, Sir, if me mum had let you?'

'That's true, Miss Pegg, but you know we all change our minds about things.'

'Are you still mad at Mum, Sir?' She wanted so desperately to be reassured.

'No, I was a bit annoyed at first, but not now. I think it is very generous of both of you to make the offer and I am grateful. Tell you what, if I need to move at any time, I'll let you know and if the room is available I'll have it. How's that?'

'That's okay, Sir.'

'Good, now we'll forget the whole thing until then, shall we?'

'Yes, Sir.'

She smiled, completely relieved. She was a good kid, and perhaps would, in due course, be able to teach her mother a few more lessons in the essential humanities.

CHAPTER 14

THE AUGUST HOLIDAY was a lazy time for me. I spent most of it in reading, visiting exhibitions, going to the theatre, ballet, and concerts. I had two letters from Gillian, who was holidaying with her mother at Geneva – gay, informative letters about places visited, sights seen, and things remembered and waiting to be shared. It would be wonderful to see her again.

When the new term began nearly half the class was absent, away in the hop-fields of Kent with other members of their families. This was a routine, annual affair, a kind of working holiday in the country. Most of the moving spirits in the class were away and the others felt a bit lost, evidently missing them and as anxious for their return as I was.

Pamela was back at school, but seemed a somewhat changed girl. She was quiet, moody, aloof, and showed no wish to participate in the midday dance sessions which were once her favourite interest. I assumed that she was missing Barbara Pegg who was away in the hop-fields with her mother, and hoped that soon everything would be as before.

By the third week of September they were back, and, as I had hoped, much of the old spirit was soon re-established. They told me about the fun and games they had had on holiday, of the money they had earned and the things they hoped to buy with it. Barbara Pegg was back and I expected that Pamela would quickly throw off the blues which seemed to have settled rather heavily on her, but, though she smiled occasionally, she remained wrapped tightly in some mysterious brooding disaffection, which seemed to take from her that wonderful vitality which I had so much admired.

She fell into the habit of remaining in the classroom during recess, and doing lots of little things for me without being asked, showing a strange aptitude for anticipating my wishes. She would keep my table tidy and fetch a cup of tea from the staffroom. Clinty laughingly complained that the girls were keeping me away from the women, and though I protested, it was true that each recess found me surrounded by a large group of my class, boys and girls, who never seemed to tire of asking me more and more questions about myself, and telling me about their homes, interests and hopes for the future. The realisation that only about three months of school life remained to them stimulated their interest in everything.

I was introduced, *in absentia*, to most of the members of their families and very soon I learned of the new job 'our Joannie' had secured; of the girl 'our Alf' was going steady with; of the difficulties at home since 'our Dad' was on strike at the Docks; when 'our Mum' was expecting the new baby. I was part of it and very happy to be so much a part of it.

Sometimes I'd arrive in the morning to find a small parcel of wedding or birthday cake on my desk, always addressed simply to 'Sir'; then at recess the child concerned would tell me all about it, whether it was from herself or some other member of the family. I was always expected to eat the piece of cake then and there with my cup of tea.

Pamela was always there, just on the edge of things, listening, observant and silent. She seemed to have become overnight a grown woman; her hair no longer hung down in a pony-tail but was carefully plaited in two large braids which were in turn carefully fixed at the back of her head in an attractive bun. Her grave expression added a certain dignity to every movement. I felt that I could probably help her if I only knew what the matter was, but I could not intrude on her privacy, and I decided to wait until she got over it or some occasion presented itself for me to help. They mattered to me, all these children, and anything which bothered any one of them bothered me too.

One morning during recess Denham brought a new football to me; with him were Potter, Fernman, Jackson and Seales.

'Please, Sir, will you help us to lace this up? Mr Weston promised to attend to it for us but now he says he's too busy.'

The way in which they put a request always amused me; it seemed to suggest there could be no question of my refusing. They came to me with the complete assurance that whatever the case was I'd be agreeable and helpful. There was no denying them.

'Okay Denham, let's have it.'

The girls wandered away to leave us men with our work; only Pamela remained, somewhat apart. We pumped the ball hard, and while two of the boys held it firmly down on the table I laced it up tightly. In threading the thong through the last eyelet hole, however, the steel lacer slipped and made a small wound on my finger, from which the blood slowly trickled.

'Blimey, red blood!'

Potter's large friendly face wore a look of simulated surprise, and the other boys burst into laughter at his goggle-eyed stare, Pamela moved over quickly to Potter.

'What did you expect, fat boy? Ink?' she hissed at him, and calmly, disdainfully, she walked away to sit straight and aloof in her seat.

'Cor!' Denham gasped at the sheer venom of her attack.

Seales and Fernman merely stared from Potter to Pamela and back again, wordless with surprise. Poor Potter was flushed with embarrassment and stammered:

'I didn't mean anything, Sir; what I meant was, your colour is only skin deep, Sir.'

'Quite so, Potter,' I replied, wanting to say something to show I felt no resentment at his jovial remark. 'All colour is only skin deep.'

I finished the lacing and opened the drawer of my table to

find the strip of Elastoplast I kept there. I was annoyed with Pamela for the unnecessary and quite vehement attack on Potter, but could think of nothing I could do about it without worsening an already delicate situation.

The boys walked over to Pamela, who observed their approach with cool unconcern.

'What's up with youse?' Denham planted himself squarely in front of her, and stuck his jaw forward belligerently.

'Are you addressing me, Denham?'

'Yes.' Pamela watched him and waited.

'All right, Miss Dare then. What's up with you?'

'I don't know what you mean, Denham.' She was cool, taunting.

'Pots was only being funny, and you had to go for him like that, and right in front of Sir. What did you want to call him "fat boy" for?'

'He's fat, isn't he?'

Pamela's gaze shifted from Denham to Potter and traversed him from top to toe.

'I was only having a little joke and Sir didn't mind,' Potter offered, lamely, quailing under Pamela's examination.

At this, Pamela rose in one fierce, fluid motion. Eyes blazing, she stood straight before Potter and in her anger seemed to tower above him, her voice thick with emotion.

'Doesn't mind? How do you know he doesn't mind? Because he's decent about it and never lets on? Daft, that's what you are, the lot of youse, daft, stupid, soft!'

I sat down and watched, mesmerised by the concentrated anger of this red-headed Fury, who seemed to grow larger as she continued, her eyes boring into the helpless Potter.

'How would you like it if they were always on to you, fat Potter? Idiots, that's what you are, idiots! My life, the silly things you ask!' She screwed up her face and fell into scathing mimicry:

'Do you ever wash, Sir? Do you feel the cold, Sir? Do you ever have a haircut, Sir? Stupid, that's what you are, all of youse.'

'Coo, good old Pamela!' exclaimed Tich Jackson.

Pamela swung around to fix him with her eyes, but Tich quickly altered it to:

'I mean, Miss Dare.'

'Sir said we could ask him anything we liked, didn't he?' persisted Denham. He was unable to match Pamela's quick cutting intelligence, but he stood firm, trying to cope with one idea at a time.

'You shut up, Denham. Call that asking questions, always on about his colour and that? Can't think of anything else to ask about?'

As if unwilling to spare any of them she suddenly turned on Seales, who had, as usual, been playing the part of interested bystander.

'And you, you ought to know better.'

'Steady on, what have I done? I didn't say anything.' He sounded rather alarmed.

'You never say anything. You're coloured too, but you just sit back and keep your mouth shut. Are you scared of this lot?'

She was wonderful, tremendous in her scorn and towering anger: Boadicea revivified, flame-haired, majestic. Seales watched her for a moment, with a patience that made him centuries older than the virago before him.

'I really don't think they meant any harm, Miss Dare. When they ask questions they're only trying to find out about things they don't understand.'

Pamela was not to be mollified. 'Then why don't they ask you if they're so keen to find out?'

'I'm not Sir, Miss Dare, I only wish I was.'

Denham tried once more to make his point. 'Sir doesn't need you to stick up for him. Who do you think you are?'

'I'm not sticking up for him,' Pamela flared, 'I'm just sick and tired with all your silly remarks. And who I think I am is none of your business, Mr ruddy Denham. Red blood, indeed!' She used scorn as incisively as a surgeon's scalpel.

Potter turned away, calling over his shoulder: 'Come on, fellers, let's go down; she's crackers, she is.'

They turned to follow him and had reached the door when

Denham, struck with a sudden thought, retraced his steps and said in a hoarse whisper:

'Know what's eating you, you're stuck on Sir, that's what.'

Without waiting for her reply, he rushed through the door, leaving it to slam loudly behind him. Pamela remained standing where she was, mouth open, gazing at the closed door; then she looked towards my desk and our eyes met. I may have looked as foolishly surprised as I felt, for she blushed deeply and rushed through the door.

So there it was. Somewhere deep inside of me I had known it all along but had refused to acknowledge it, because, in spite of her full body and grown-up attitude, she was to me a child, and one who was in my care. I could appreciate that the emotional stirrings within her might be serious and important to her – it was not uncommon for girls of fifteen to be engaged or even married – but though I liked and admired her, she was to me only one of my class, and I felt a fatherly responsibility for her as for all the others. If Denham's remark was evidence of a general feeling about it, things might be a bit sticky, but he had blurted it out so suddenly that I guessed it was merely an impulsive shot in the dark. I needed to discuss this with someone. Not Gillian, because that would mean I would have to acknowledge the truth of her warning, and I was in no mood to hear her say 'I told you so.' Grace. Yes, she would be able to advise me in this, for, coming from the same background and stock, she had considerable understanding of the problems of these girls.

When Grace returned from the dining hall that afternoon I whispered to her that I wished to see her privately, and together we went up to her classroom. She listened without interruption until I had finished; then she said:

'Well, Rick, are you surprised?'

'Look, Grace, this is no time for jokes. I need advice because this thing is quite outside my experience.'

'I'm not joking, Rick. This sort of thing happens all the time wherever there are men teachers and girl students, from the Infants, right through to High School and University. Here, sit down and let me bring you up to date.'

We made ourselves comfortable and she continued:

'There hasn't been a really good man teacher in this school for ages – I'm not including the Old Man. We've been having a procession of all types. The fellows these girls have seen here have been, on the whole, scruffy, untidy men who can't be bothered to brush their teeth or their shoes, let alone do something about their shapeless ill-fitting clothes. Good God, those twerps tootle off to a training college and somehow acquire a certificate, a licence to teach, and then they appear in a classroom looking like last week's left-overs!'

In her vehemence she had risen and was walking up and down, her arms folded tightly across her bosom. Now she stopped in front of me.

'Then along comes Mr Rick Braithwaite. His clothes are well cut, pressed and neat; clean shoes, shaved, teeth sparkling, tie and handkerchief matching as if he'd stepped out of a ruddy bandbox. He's big and broad and handsome. Good God, man, what the hell else did you expect? You're so different from their fathers and brothers and neighbours. And they like you; you treat them like nice people for a change. When they come up here for cookery or needlework all I hear from them is "Sir this, Sir that, Sir said, Sir said" until I'm damn near sick of the sound of it.'

Grace had got quite worked up as she was speaking. I had not seen her show so much emotion before.

'You see, Rick,' she went on, 'I've known these kids a long time, been teaching here nearly twenty years. I've seen many of them as nippers in their prams, so I know all about them and I like them, every one of the snotty-nosed little bastards. You've made good on this job, Rick. Only the other day the Old Man was saying the same thing to me. You treat them with kindness and courtesy and what's more they're learning a lot with you. Be patient with Pamela. She's only just finding out that she's a grown woman, and you're probably the first real man she's met. Be tactful and I'm sure she'll soon pull herself together.'

I got up and moved towards the door. I had been given more than I had asked for, and I felt humble and grateful.

'Thanks for the chat, Grace, you've been very helpful.'

'Come and see Auntie Grace any time you've got troubles,' she laughed.

I was halfway through the door when she said, as if in afterthought, 'I like Miss Blanchard, don't you?' I turned away without replying.

Grace was right. The emotional outburst must have released some of the tension building up inside Pamela, for in a little while she seemed to throw off some of her aloofness and bad temper, and once again entered into the community spirit within the classroom and at the midday dances. Now and then I would notice a look of worry on her face, but I could see nothing to account for it and hoped it would soon disappear altogether.

Recently, Mr Florian had fallen into the habit of dropping in on us and entering into our discussions, thus adding to them the benefit of his wide and varied interests and experiences. It was a treat to have him there, perched on the side of one of the children's desks with his arms clasped about his knees, his eyes shining with delight as he spoke or argued with them, prodding, cajoling, encouraging them to express their own views in a clear and fearless manner. He was like a favourite visiting uncle with a pocketful of surprises. I rather suspected that many of them would have liked to hug him, such was their feeling for him.

Sometimes he would divide the class into two opposing factions to debate the pros and cons of some idea or other which either affected their lives now or would be of importance later on. Mr Florian acted as leader of one faction and I led the other. The arguments that followed were lively, entertaining and enlightening. Youngsters who might be thought backward because of failure to win entrance to a Grammar school or even to some other local secondary school, were exhibiting a degree of careful analysis which, though expressed without rigid observation for the rules of syntax, could not easily be bettered by many other children with greater advantages. Here indeed was a vindication of this man's beliefs and of the soundness of the concepts on which he acted. They wore no school uniform, but they possessed character and confidence and an ability to speak up for themselves. They might not be familiar with the declension of Greek or Latin verbs, but they were ready, or nearly so, to meet the stern realities which awaited them a few short months away.

CHAPTER 15

ONE MORNING IN October, soon after assembly, I was called to the Head's office and found him looking grave and troubled. He told me that one of my class, Patrick Fernman, had been arrested by the police the night before on a charge of wounding another boy with a flick-knife during a scuffle. The wounded boy, a tough little tyro in Miss Phillips' class, was in hospital seriously ill, so much so that an emergency operation had been necessary immediately upon his admission.

Fernman was on remand and would remain in custody until he was brought before the Magistrates at the Juvenile Court next Monday. It was now Thursday. The Head wished me to prepare a report on the boy's attendance, conduct, abilities and interests.

'This is very serious, isn't it, Sir?'

'Yes, Braithwaite, more serious than you think. The wounding is bad enough, but both boys are from this school and Greenslade does not exactly occupy a very high place in the Magistrates' opinion; they have on occasion criticised our attitude towards punishment, and have not hesitated to infer that this school is very nearly a breeding ground for delinquents. Any appearance of a member of our school before them is further grist to their mill.'

'Have any of them visited this school?'

'Oh yes, one of them even has some personal association with us. But you must not misunderstand my remarks; I do not suggest that because of their views about the school there will be any contravention of justice. But it would help enormously if we had a little more help and understanding of our efforts in such official quarters. We would like them to appreciate the fact that we fill a very urgent need among these children, possibly because they could so very easily be delinquents.'

'Is there anything else I can do?'

'I don't think so; not yet at any rate.'

'What about his parents? Would a visit to them do any good?'

He thought about it for a while, then said: 'I can't see that it would do any harm. I'll write a personal note to them and you can take it along when you go.'

I left him and returned to my class. They were working quietly and I somehow felt that they knew all about Fernman; yet none of them so much as mentioned his name or gave any hint of having noticed his absence. At the least hint of trouble they, like their elders, promptly closed their ranks, and in a time such as this even I was an outsider.

I prepared the report, and if I laid rather much emphasis on the boy's credits, I felt justified because I knew him to be a fine, sensitive, intelligent boy in spite of everything. The wounded youth, Bobby Ellis, was a rugged thirteen-year-old who considered himself very tough, bullied his smaller colleagues, embarrassed and annoyed the girls by his precocious, unwelcome attentions and had even once tried conclusions with Potter and received a good cuffing for his pains. Although I did not condone or excuse Fernman's use of a knife, I felt sure that he must have been driven to such an extreme by some vicious attack by the young bully.

At lunch I told Gillian what had happened and she offered to accompany me to see the Fernmans, who lived in a neat walk-up flat in Jubilee Street. When the mother answered our ring her face bore the tell-tale marks of prolonged weeping. She led us into a small comfortable sitting-room and we introduced ourselves and were in turn introduced to the father and grandmother of the boy, all of whom wore the same expressions of deep sorrow. Mr Fernman read the

Headmaster's letter and asked us to convey the family's appreciation and gratitude. Then, to the accompaniment of quiet weeping by the two women, he told us the story.

The knife was one of Grandma Fernman's prized possessions. She used it for cutting away tiny shreds of knotted silk during her weaving. It was always kept razor-sharp by a barber at Shadwell, and it was Patrick's job to take it there whenever it required attention. Apparently he had unwisely shown the knife in its velvet-lined case to Bobby Ellis, but had refused to let him touch it. An argument followed, and the young bully had tried to take it forcibly. He was as tall as and huskier than Patrick and did not hesitate to try every roughneck trick he knew; the case was smashed in the struggle and somehow Patrick had seized the knife and used it, cutting his own hand quite deeply in the process.

Thoroughly frightened by the sight of the blood and the shrill screams of the wounded boy, Patrick had left him and run off home, quite hysterical from shock and the pain of his own wound. He was quickly taken to a nearby chemist where his wound was dressed, and then Mr Fernman had insisted on taking him to the police. The boy, Ellis, meanwhile had been taken to hospital by a passing motorist.

The incident had shaken the small household to its foundations; they were evidently a very close-knit Jewish family. I assured them that we at Greenslade were all deeply shocked and grieved at the incident, but would do all we could for Patrick, who had always proved himself friendly, co-operative and trustworthy. I mentioned that I had prepared his school report and this was some small consolation to them. Gillian was comforting in a way which made me very glad that she had come. She spoke to the unhappy mother in Yiddish, an accomplishment I had never suspected she possessed, and before we left it was quite clear that she had completely won them by her charm and sweetness. This girl was no dilettante playing at Lady Bountiful; she was earnest and honestly sympathetic, and these simple folk, who so well understand such things, warmed to her.

The next morning I asked the Headmaster if I might be permitted to attend the court hearing on the following Monday. I wanted to see and hear at first hand how the Law dealt with young offenders, and to note the way in which the offenders themselves behaved when faced with the Law's solemn majesty.

I arrived at the Juvenile Courts soon after ten o'clock on the Monday morning. The large waiting room was crowded with parents and their children, whose ages were from about six to sixteen, and whose offences, I later discovered, ranged from non-attendance at school to shop-breaking and charges involving sexual misconduct. I explained my business to one of the policemen in attendance and waited while he sought permission for me to enter the courtroom.

Fernman was standing in a corner of the waiting room with his parents and grandmother. He and they looked dejected and miserable, in contrast to the brash, cocky attitude of some others of about his age, or the innocent unconcern of the little ones who were happily unaware of the gravity of the situations going on around them. I did not go over to him: these Cockneys are proud people and prefer to be left to themselves at times when they feel ashamed.

Inside the courtroom I was struck by the absence of the ponderous formality and the trappings usually associated with the machinery of the Law. It was a small square room, in the centre of which trestle-tables covered with coarse woollen cloth were arranged to form three sides of a hollow square; on the fourth side were a few rows of chairs for the parents and guardians of the children concerned.

The magistrates, one man and two women, occupied the centre table and were flanked by the Clerk of the Court on one side and the Court Bailiff on the other. Representatives of various of the Council's Child Welfare departments were seated nearby busily preparing and arranging stacks of documents pertinent to the cases listed for hearing that day. Several policemen and policewomen were grouped near the door.

The first case concerned a girl of about fourteen, pink-cheeked, full-figured and somewhat defiant. A young policewoman stepped forward and read the charge in the kind of stilted monotonous voice which aims more at enunciating each word separately and clearly than in conveying sense.

This was the second hearing of the case, the girl having meanwhile been in a remand home while certain investigations were made into her background. The charge stated that she had had carnal knowledge and was considered to be in need of care and protection.

It transpired that the girl had been on intimate terms with several youths in the same tenement building in Stepney and was now pregnant, with no certainty as to the person actually responsible.

She listened tight-lipped to the details of her misfortunes, looking younger but far wiser than the prim uniformed girl who read the charge; an expectant mother at fourteen, betrayed by the combined evils of poverty and overcrowding and ignorance, and abandoned by an unforgiving aunt who sat stiff in her outraged respectability and inflexible in her resolve to have nothing more to do with her wayward charge. The girl did not seem unduly impressed by the proceedings: probably she had not yet completely understood the extent of her trouble, and I felt sure that the terms in which the charge was couched were too unfamiliar to mean much to her. The actual machinery of the court was intended to be as informal as possible, yet the terminology used was vague and involved. 'Carnal knowledge', I thought, what an odd-sounding term. The act itself was simple enough in the circumstances; could not simpler, more understandable references to it be used, for the children's sake?

The Chairman of the bench looked large and formidable, his shaggy grey brows beetling as he listened to the unhappy story. Then, after a whispered consultation with his associates, he addressed the girl in a surprisingly gentle voice.

'Do you understand everything that has just been read, my dear?'

'Yes.'

'Is there anything you would like to say?'

'No.'

'Do you realise that by your behaviour you have caused your aunt a great deal of sorrow?'

The girl merely shrugged. Her aunt's state of mind was of no interest to her whatever.

The Chairman asked an official for the school report, which described the girl as intelligent, hardworking, friendly and helpful; her grades were high, her attendance excellent. But that was not enough. In my mind's eye I replaced her at random with the girls in my class, most of whom would have a similarly good report. Yet, what did I really know of them, of their lives away from school, of the pressures attendant upon the early physical development in which they took so much interest and pride? The area was not without its prostitutes, pimps and other specialists in illicit persuasion. What could I as a teacher do to counteract such influences? The unlucky ones were found out and sometimes exposed like this girl; but what of the others? Who could tell what was going on in the minds of youngsters on the threshold of adulthood; where did childhood end and adulthood begin when you are at school today, and tomorrow at work as junior assistant breadwinner to an overlarge family? If they were old enough to earn, why should they not consider themselves old enough to learn and do other things which adults do? And what would happen if they were encouraged to try ways and means of acquiring much more money, quicker and with less effort?

History and Geography, Arithmetic and Religious Education, were they enough? I talked to them about life, but in deference to their youth and inexperience I spoke objectively, giving to certain important matters of sex a remoteness, in the absurd hope that my remarks would neither cause offence nor be unduly distorted or misrepresented. Was I somehow failing them, contenting myself with their apparent 'niceness' and favourable reaction and conduct to myself?

'Well, my dear, your aunt is not prepared to have you back, so you'll be sent to live in a special home where you'll be treated well until your baby is born.'

The Chairman's voice showed real fatherly concern; years of experience had taught him to look behind the brash, sulking, defiant exteriors and see the fear, the panic, the helplessness of youngsters like her, whose only crime was ignorance. The girl left the room accompanied by a matronly court official.

Several other cases were dealt with before Fernman's name was called. He entered the room slightly ahead of his parents, his right hand in a sling, his head hung in utter dejection. He stood before the bench while behind him his relatives sat in a tight, unhappy little group on the hard chairs. A policeman read the preliminary statement, intoning each word as if it were written in a foreign language; then he itemised the various charges made against the boy.

1. Being in possession of an offensive weapon, to wit an eight-inch knife.
2. Wounding with intent to commit bodily harm.
3. Malicious wounding.

The knife was exhibited to the bench, and from my point of vantage I must admit it seemed an attractive and innocent-looking article. Fernman looked sickly pale as the policeman described the victim's wound and the injury Fernman himself had sustained to his hand. Now and then the Clerk of the Court would interrupt the policeman's report to enquire more closely into some detail of it.

Transcripts of the charge and of Fernman's school report were handed around the bench.

'Has he been in any previous trouble?' the Chairman of Magistrates asked.

A probation officer rose and stepped forward.

'No previous record, Sir. The other boy, the victim of the attack, appeared in this court last month before you; that case of the boy who burnt his mother with the hot poker. He's under a supervision order for one calendar year.'

'How long is he likely to be in hospital?'

'The doctor said it would be about six weeks, Sir.'

'Thank you.'

The Chairman then turned to Fernman, who seemed ready to drop.

'You are charged with a most serious offence; it is only by extreme good luck that the charge is not much more serious. According to the reports, a little more push, a little more pressure and today you would be facing a charge of murder.'

The poor boy shook visibly; his tongue kept flicking out across his lips vainly trying to moisten them. The vigilant policeman moved over to him, then said to the Chairman: 'Could he be allowed to sit, Sir? He seems to be a bit all in.'

'Yes, give him a chair.' The voice was chill. The Chairman spoke briefly with the woman colleague on each side of him, then picked up the knife very gingerly by its ornate handle; the blade, safely retracted within the polished wood, was not in sight.

'In this country we specially dislike and deplore the use of this type of thing. I would be happy if I could be told that the Government had taken some steps to ban the sale of such articles in these islands. It is a vicious weapon at best, and in the hands of a foolish, inexperienced youth its danger is increased immeasurably.'

Again he paused to let his hearers digest the profundity and weight of his remarks.

'A parent who would allow a child to play with an unexploded bomb would receive and be deserving of our most severe condemnation. It is our considered opinion that in many ways an object like' – and here he suddenly pressed the button on the handle to release a slim, shining, wicked-looking blade about eight inches long, which leaped out of its polished housing with a soft 'ping' – 'an object like this is no less dangerous in the hands of a boy. Had this weapon been used to greater effect, resulting in a more serious charge, no amount of tears would have been able to restore that life.'

Now all informality vanished from the little courtroom as the clear, vibrant voice rose and fell in measured delivery. Here was the Law at work, as dignified, severe and remote as its representative who seemed to grow larger and graver as he spoke.

'The court has read and heard the statements of the boy and his parents, and we are in no doubt that this youth did not arm himself with the weapon, but was sent out to have it sharpened; a simple enough errand one might think, but one which had serious consequences. When faced with the danger of attack, especially if such attack is from someone or something felt to possess greater physical strength, or which is able in some way to inspire a high degree of fear, some people are prone to rely on some form of weapon in an attempt to control the situation. That same fear may be so great in intensity that the weapon is used with greater force and to a more damaging extent than might have been intended.

'I want to warn you, Patrick Fernman, and to advise you against the use of weapons, any type of weapons. This frightening experience should be a severe lesson to you and to your unhappy parents.'

Then the Chairman turned his attention to Fernman's school. He did not mention it by name, but to anyone familiar with the area there could be no doubt that he meant Greenslade. His voice was harsh and cuttingly sarcastic as he referred to the evils of 'free discipline' in general and the particular practice of it at 'a certain school in this vicinity'. In his opinion such schools were the brood-pens of delinquency, attested by the frequency with which children, boys and girls, from that school appeared before the Juvenile Courts on one charge or another.

He felt that certain cranks and dreamers were doing more harm than good to the youth of the area by pursuing an educational course which over the years of trial had achieved nothing to recommend it; rather it had encouraged among the young a vicious licence to do evil, and a continued disregard for established social institutions.

'Those people,' continued the Chairman, 'to whom the education and development of these youths is entrusted, cannot hope to escape the final responsibility for the natural result of their ill-conceived schemes. I sometimes am persuaded that justice would be better served if they were made to answer the charges for the offences which, one might say, they have by proxy committed.'

He turned his attention once more to the boy, who had sat bemused and silent at this angry tirade; this time, however, the voice was kindly and rather paternal. He told Fernman that he was sure that his own evident grief and the sorrow which he had brought to his parents was punishment enough; however, for his own good, a supervision order would be made which would require that he report to a probation officer once weekly for a period of one year. He then discharged the boy into his parents' keeping, and the little group left the court, reunited and trying to smile through their tears of relief.

After a reasonable interval to allow them to leave without the embarrassment of having to talk to me, I left the courtroom. I did not for a moment agree with the Chairman's scathing denunciations, but nevertheless I was conscious of a feeling of increased responsibility for the young people who were in my care for nearly six hours each day.

CHAPTER 16

FOR ABOUT A week Fernman was quiet and withdrawn. He could not write because of his damaged right hand, so he sat reading most of the time, or listening with interest to our discussions, though making no contribution to them. But gradually the natural warmth of his personality reasserted itself, and soon he was taking his full share in our activities again.

About this time, with the Head's permission, several evening visits were arranged. We went to Sadler's Wells for a performance of *Coppélia*; to the Old Vic to see Laurence Olivier in *Hamlet*; and, as a change, we went to Wembley Stadium to see the famous Harlem Globetrotters basketball team in action.

For these trips we bore the expenses ourselves. Days before each projected visit we would estimate the total cost of the tickets and coach transport, and the amount each person would need to contribute. Then one of the class would be responsible for collecting the money in easy stages, checking carefully to avoid mistakes. None of them ever wished to be left out, and the Head and I saw to it that inability to raise the required amount did not prevent anyone from making the trip. On most occasions we found it more convenient to hire a coach, so that the group was kept together at all times, making supervision easy.

Because of this arrangement many of the staff were pleased to join us, the more so as the various theatre managements granted us special prices for the party. They, too, soon felt the full impact of the change in the youngsters. Before visiting the theatre the children and I would discuss the ballet or play, with reference to the general background against which it was presented, and any features of historical or social interest which might be likely to arise. On the way back they would give full rein to their critical intelligence, and often presented new and interesting points of view on old and familiar things. They were quick to appreciate and recognise the various art forms as part of their national heritage, equally available to themselves as to all others. At such times I could have wished that some of those who most loudly declaimed against the school and its policies could be with us, attentive but invisible.

The visit to Wembley was different in many ways. The Globetrotters were a skilful and highly trained team who combined a slick proficiency with admirable showmanship; their handling of the ball at times bordered on wizardry, and they kept the crowd either spell-bound at their speed and accuracy or shrieking with laughter at their smooth clowning over the discomfiture of their luckless opponents.

The children laughed themselves hoarse, and on the way back were still rocking at the remembering of this or that amusing incident. Next day I was closely questioned about the team and its members. The children were somewhat surprised to learn that some had been college or University men; their vision of the American Negro, being so largely based on films, did not include high intellectual attainment. However, through discussion, I believe that slowly they were beginning to see all mankind from a new standpoint of essential dignity.

One morning the Headmaster came to my classroom soon after recess.

'There's a lady in my office asking to speak to you,' he whispered, standing with his back to the class to avoid being overheard. 'As you know, I never allow parents access to the staff, but she has told me the reason for wanting to see you and I think you would be doing her a service by doing so. I will stay with your class until you return.'

I walked into the Head's office and saw a tall, smartly

dressed woman standing by the window gazing out into the opposite churchyard. As soon as she turned to me I knew who she was: the same brilliant auburn hair and fresh complexion, the same proud bearing – Mrs Dare, Pamela's mother.

We shook hands and sat facing each other.

'I'm Mr Braithwaite. The Head said you wanted to see me.'

'Yes, Sir, it's about my girl, Pamela. I'm Mrs Dare.'

I suddenly felt nervous. What on earth did she want to see me about?

'I'm very worried about her, Sir, and wondered if you would help by speaking to her. She'll take notice of what you say, Sir, she always does.'

I could hardly believe my ears; relief flowed pleasantly through me, relief and pleasure.

'Why, Mrs Dare? What's the trouble?'

Her handsome face was pale and troubled.

'She's been staying out late, Sir, been coming in after eleven some nights. She won't tell me where she goes or what she does and it's worrying me. She's a big girl, you know what I mean, Sir, and anything could happen, I just don't know what to do.' Her lips were trembling as she strove to control herself; the gloves of silk mesh were twisted between her strong fingers.

'But what can I do, Mrs Dare? I'm only her teacher, you know. Perhaps Mr Florian. . . . '

'No, Sir,' she interrupted, 'I think she'd listen to you if you tell her to come in early. I know what she thinks of you, Sir. When her friends are over at the house I hear them talking about what you do and what you say, and she's always on about what you think and that.'

'Won't her father do something?'

'Jim's dead, Sir, died in 1943 when Pam was just over eight. Tail-gunner in the Air Force he was, shot down over Germany. You were in the Air Force too, Sir, weren't you?'

'Yes, Mrs Dare.'

'So Pam said. She misses her dad, Sir, and I think she sort of looks up to you. Please have a word with her, Sir.'

She was very near to tears. I stood up, quickly assured her that I would do my best, and showed her out.

As I entered the classroom Mr Florian walked over to me.
'Has she left?'

'Yes, I've just seen her to the door.'

'Will you do it?'

'Well, Sir, I seem to have no choice.'

'I think you should, not only because of the mother, but for the girl's sake. Have a word with her, here, or in my office if you like. After school would be best.' And with that he left me.

As the children were leaving for dinner I beckoned Pamela aside and told her I wanted to speak to her after school that day. She did not appear surprised at my request.

'Has my mum been here, Sir?'

'Yes, she has been to see me.'

'All right, Sir.'

'Look here, Miss Dare, if you'd rather I didn't interfere you've only to say so.'

'Oh, no, Sir, I don't mind.'

'Fine, then we'll have a chat here after school.'

While Gillian and I were having our sandwiches in the staff-room, I told her of the morning's events; she was silent for a while after I had finished.

'You're really involved with these children, aren't you?'

'I suppose we're all involved with them, one way or another.'

'You're more involved with them than most.'

'What about you?'

'Least of all me. For me this is merely a way of occupying myself for the time being; I've no "sense of vocation" as Mrs Drew calls it.'

'Neither have I. It was by the merest accident that I entered this profession. Remind me to tell you the whole sad story one rainy day.'

'If I'm with you on a rainy day, no sad stories, please. Anyway, they matter to you.'

'Yes, and to the Old Man, and Clinty and Grace and Mrs Drew and all the rest of us.'

'Not quite all of us. Josy Dawes and her girlfriend matter only to each other.'

'They're rather odd, those two.'

'That's putting it mildly, there are other words which more aptly describe that sort of thing.'

I looked at her, surprised; that interpretation of the conduct of those two had not occurred to me.

'Good Lord, do you really think so?'

'What else is there for me to think? They're always whispering little confidences to each other and surreptitiously holding hands. It's unhealthy to say the least, and bad for the children.'

'But they're both good teachers, don't you agree?'

'Oh well, I suppose one should be grateful for small mercies, and they're not harming anyone.'

'You're involved with these children too, whether you care to admit it or not. Your remarks just now betrayed you.'

'Oh, well!' She was smiling now. 'I can never convince you about that, I'm sure. Anyway, you be careful, especially with the Dare girl; that's no schoolgirl crush she has on you. I've watched her and I know. She's a woman and the sooner you realise it, the better. Don't make the mistake of treating her like a child, whatever you do.'

'Okay, I won't.'

The others returned from lunch in a group. As soon as they were inside the room Weston remarked:

'Saw Pamela Dare's mother around here this morning. What's up, Braithwaite?'

'Why should something be up?'

'Something's always up when these people are about. They're never seen around here except to complain about something or other.'

'Was anything the matter, Rick?' Clinty enquired with mild interest.

'No, she must have been to see the Old Man.' I did not want to discuss the matter.

'Quite a dish, isn't she?' chirped Clinty.

'Ask Weston,' I replied, 'he claims to have seen her.'

He seemed pleased to be brought back into the conversation and remarked:

'I suppose some men would find her attractive.'

'Once again the emphasis being on the word "men", eh Weston?'

Clinty dearly loved to bait him, but I entertained no pity for this hulking, bushy-faced fellow.

At the end of the afternoon Pamela went out with the others, but returned a few minutes later. She brought a chair to my table and sat down, staring straight ahead through the open window.

'Well, Miss Dare, your mother seems to be very worried about you.'

'Please Sir, couldn't you call me Pamela?' It was a quiet, sincere request.

'All right, Pamela. Your mother says you've been staying out rather late.'

'I've been going to me nan's, Sir.'

'And staying so late?'

'It's not far, Sir, just around the corner from where we live.'

'Then why didn't you tell your mother where you went?'

'Mum doesn't really care about me, Sir. All she cares about is her friends.'

'You know that's not true. Why did she come here to see me?' Pamela said nothing. 'Is there anything wrong, Pamela? Are you worried about anything here?'

She shook her head, then said: 'Not about the work or anything like that, Sir, but some of the other kids are always talking and gossiping about me. I always know when they're . . . when it's me they're talking about, most of them, even Babs, Sir.'

'But why should you think they're talking about you, Pamela? Has something happened? Are you in any kind of trouble?'

Again she shook her head, and stared past me through the window. I felt uncomfortable, and unwilling to ask her anything which might embarrass her. Although she had willingly agreed to this meeting, I had no wish to intrude on her privacy, for she was a young woman and I did not really know what to say to her. 'Miss Dare, I mean Pamela, if you'd rather I did not interfere, you've only to say so.'

'Oh no, Sir, it's not that.'

Slowly it came out, the whole sad story.

After the death of Mr Dare, Pamela and her mother had found comfort in the company of each other, going everywhere and doing things together, so that as the girl grew up they were more like two sisters than mother and daughter. Mrs Dare worked as a shop assistant in the City, and soon Pamela was old enough to help with the household chores. This idyllic relationship had continued until very recently, when several men friends had started to call on the attractive widow. The neighbours had begun to gossip.

Things had come to a head during the holidays. Something had occurred which had seriously upset the girl, but about this she remained silent.

'Have you tried to tell your mother how you feel about these things?'

'At first, Sir, but she never listened, so I didn't bother any more.'

'Doesn't your nan know that your being late would upset your mother?'

'Sometimes Mum's very late coming home, and Nan thinks I should not be in the house all by myself.'

'Well, Pamela, there seems to be no way in which I can help.'

'Wouldn't you come and talk with Mum, Sir?'

'Would that help?'

'I think it might, Sir.'

'Very well then. When will she be at home?'

'About quarter past six, Sir.'

'Fine. Will you tell her I'll be around then?'

'Yes, Sir.' For the first time she smiled, then replaced the chair and left.

I went to the staffroom to fetch my coat. Gillian was sitting there waiting for me.

'Well?'

'I'm seeing her mother this evening.'

'Why?'

'Pamela has some idea it will help if I have a word with both of them.'

126

'Where are you seeing them?'

'At her home.'

'Is that wise?'

'I don't know, Gillian, but I hope so, I sincerely hope so.'

She was silent for a few moments, then she said:

'Are you thinking of remaining at Greenslade long, Rick?'

'I suppose so. Actually it hadn't occurred to me to leave it. Why?'

'You could easily get a job in a better school. Everyone agrees you're a fine teacher. It would be a pity to stay here.'

'I've only just begun teaching, you know, not more than a few months. It hardly seems enough to decide whether or not I'm really much good at it.'

'Such modesty!'

'No, I'm serious. I may be able to get to terms with these kids, but it might be quite different with others. I think I ought to stay where I am and learn a little more about the job and my own abilities before I think of moving.' I looked at my watch. 'Look at the time, I'm afraid I must go now.'

'Do be careful, Rick.'

'I will. 'Bye.'

''Bye, Rick.'

Like so many other women of this area, Mrs Dare and Pamela kept their home spotlessly clean. Pamela opened the door to me, and as I greeted her mother I was conscious of the strain under which both of them were living just then. When we had seated ourselves I said:

'Mrs Dare, Pamela felt that it might help if I came along and had a chat with you. She has not told me much and if you feel I should not interfere I won't mind.'

Now that I was here I was rather anxious to get it over with as quickly as possible. I had the feeling that I was intruding unnecessarily in the lives of these people on the very weak excuse of my position as the girl's teacher.

'Oh, no, Mr Braithwaite.' Then, turning to her daughter, she said: 'Pam, will you go and fix some tea; I'd like to talk to Sir alone.'

Dear me, I thought, even the mothers are falling into the 'Sir' habit. Pamela obediently left us, and Mrs Dare began:

'I guess it's all my fault really. I've let Pam down.'

'In what way, Mrs Dare?' If I had to hear about it, the sooner the better.

'It's like this. Pam had wanted for some time to go and see her dad's people at Chalkwell, so we agreed that she'd spend two weeks with them over the school holidays. She and I first went to Scarborough for a week, my holidays, you know, then I took her down to Chalkwell and came back here. I thought I'd have a few days to myself, you know how it is; I've got one or two friends and they've been taking me out sometimes. Well, Pam had been away for a week and she wrote me twice to say how much she liked it there, so I thought she was enjoying herself. On the Wednesday, I met a friend of mine and I invited him to have a cup of tea.

'Well, you know how it is, one thing led to another, and he decided to stay the night.'

She had twisted her handkerchief into an unrecognisable wreck, and her eyes filled with tears which she made no effort to stop.

'We were asleep when Pam came in. She's always had a key. She must have got homesick or something for she suddenly made up her mind to come home. She'd come in quietly to surprise me and there I was, Sir, me and my friend.'

She paused, swallowed, then continued: 'I don't know what it was but something made me open my eyes, perhaps it was the light she'd switched on. I'll never forget the look on her face, Sir, never. She looked at me and ran off to her room and locked herself in. I woke my friend up and made him get dressed and leave; then I tried to get into her room but she wouldn't answer me.' Her voice fell to a whisper and I had to lean forward to hear the rest of it.

'Next day I tried to talk to her about it, but she'd just sit and cry and not say a word. I couldn't seem to get near her, somehow.' The tears were a steady stream down her face now.

'About her staying out late, have you any idea where she went?'

'I know she goes over to her nan's, my mother, over in Grover Street, but Nan wouldn't keep her there so late.'

'Have you been to see your mother?'

'Well, no. She's not too friendly with me at the moment. People have been telling her things about me; some folks around here seem to have nothing better to do than gossip about others.'

'Pamela has got the idea that you don't care about her any more.'

'Oh, Sir, how could she think that? I've been worrying myself silly about her. She's a big girl, you know what I mean, and some people think she is much older than she is, eighteen or nineteen maybe. I thought that perhaps, because of what she's seen, she might have gone and done something silly.'

Good Lord, I thought, what am I supposed to say to all this; the more Mrs Dare told me of her difficulties, the more uncomfortable I felt. I really knew nothing about the lives of these people, for only a few short months ago I was a complete stranger both to them and to the district. What could I do now? The woman was older than myself and I did not feel either equipped or experienced enough to advise her or even her daughter on so delicate a matter. I could not see that my visit would really change anything. Pamela was, as her mother remarked, a big girl – a young woman really – and from the way she had dealt with Denham and with the two old ladies in the train, I had little doubt that she could look after herself reasonably well. Then why was I here? I looked at the mother's distraught face and remarked lamely: 'I don't think Pamela's likely to do anything silly.'

'One can't be too careful round about here, Mr Braithwaite, and with her staying out late and that, anything might happen. I came to you because I felt sure she'd stop at home if you asked her to.'

Gillian was right, I shouldn't have come. I suddenly felt angry with myself for being so short-sighted; my conceit in overestimating my importance to the children had led to this, and I was sobered by the thoughts which now crowded my mind. What would the other children think or say if they knew of my visit to Pamela's home; would Pamela tell them that I had called and what reason was she likely to give for my visit? Any chatter about a teacher and his girl students, no matter how unfounded, would be viewed unfavourably, and in the mouth of someone like Weston could assume grave proportions. The sooner I was out of this the better.

'Let's call Pamela in, shall we?' I said to Mrs Dare. I did not quite know what I'd say to her, but the idea was to say something quickly and leave; I'd try not to make this kind of mistake again. Pamela came in and sat beside her mother, and I took the plunge.

'Pamela, your mother has told me about what happened, and I think I understand how you feel, how you both feel; but in spite of that, I can't see that you are doing any good by staying out late and making your mother anxious. When you are outside the school what you do is really not my business, but as you both have asked me to intervene, let me say that I would like to feel that your behaviour outside of school is as commendable and ladylike as I have always found it in the classroom.'

I was being deliberately severe and pedagogic; she'd not want to talk about this when I was through.

'Let's put first things first. You owe your mother the duty of courtesy, much more than you do to your teachers, and I would like to feel that you are not neglectful of that duty. Most families occasionally have their problems, and they manage to solve them in due course; try not to create others unnecessarily. Remember, Pamela. I'm depending on you – we're both depending on you to play the game from now on; I don't need to tell you of the risks you run on these streets late at night.'

I stood up. I'd done what they both wanted, I supposed. 'Well, I must push off now, Mrs Dare,' I said. Then I turned to Pamela.

'Can I depend on you to let your mother know where you are whenever you think you'll be out a bit late?'

'Yes, Sir,' she replied quietly.

With that I made my adieus and left. The rest was up to

them. Mrs Dare would probably be more careful in future and Pamela would soon enough view adult conduct in different terms; but in the ensuing weeks I would keep my ear to the ground, just in case. On my way to the bus stop I made a point of keeping a sharp lookout for familiar faces, and when I was finally safely settled on the train at Liverpool Street, I breathed a prayer of thanks.

CHAPTER 17

THE HALF-YEARLY report of the Students' Council was on November 15th, and was one of the important days in the calendar of Greenslade School. I had heard quite a deal about these occasions and became as excited as the children as the day approached. It was entirely their day, arranged, presented and controlled by them. I observed the activities of my class as they prepared for it, noting with pride the business-like way in which tasks were allocated and fitted into a neat programme. There were whispered conferences with members of other classes in the arrangement of it.

On that day there was no assembly. The children arrived smartly dressed and polished, and Miss Joseph and Denham, who seemed to be the important officials for the occasion, moved about among their colleagues ensuring that each one was ready to play his (or her) part.

A bell was rung at 10.0 a.m. and everyone trooped into the auditorium to sit together in classes. Miss Joseph and Denham, the two most senior students, sat on the stage, one on each side of Mr Florian, who, as soon as everyone was seated and silent, stood and addressed the school.

He spoke at length, reiterating the aims and policy of the school and of the important contribution each child could make to the furtherance of those aims. He gave praise wherever it was indicated, but insisted that there was yet a great deal to be done, by themselves, towards a general improvement in conduct, cleanliness and the pursuit of knowledge. As I listened I realised that this man was in no way remote from his school; his remarks all showed that he identified himself with it and everyone in it. He then wished them success with the Council Meeting and left the stage to tremendous applause.

Things now moved quickly into gear. First, Miss Joseph stood up, and gave a short explanation of the Council's purpose and its activities. Each class would report, through its representatives, on the studies pursued during the half year which began after Easter, a representative having been chosen for each subject. When all the classes had completed their reports a panel of teachers would be invited to occupy the stage and answer questions from the body of the hall on matters arising out of the various reports. The selection of the panel, as with everything else, was entirely at the discretion of the children and no members of the staff knew either how many or which teachers would be invited to sit.

The reports began with the lowest or youngest class first. These were mainly twelve-year-olds who had joined the school the previous summer. Most of them were shy and rather frightened at standing up before the entire school, but nevertheless they managed it creditably; they had been newly introduced to the difficulties of seeking information for themselves, so their report was understandably rather short.

Class after class was represented, and it was obvious that with each succeeding term there was a marked development in their ability to express themselves. Much of the work was rather elementary, but to them it loomed large because they understood it and something of its relationship to themselves. Throughout all the reports, the emphasis was on what they understood rather than on what they were expected to learn.

When the turn of my class came I sat up anxiously. From the list he held in his hand, Denham called out the names of the representatives, together with the subjects on which they would report.

Potter   — Arithmetic
Sapiano   — Nature Study

Miss Pegg and Jackson — Geography
Miss Dare and Fernman— Physiology
Miss Dodd   — History
Denham   — P.T. and Games
Miss Joseph   — Domestic Science

I felt terribly pleased and proud to see the confident courtesy with which Denham used the term 'Miss' in addressing each of the senior girls; I felt sure that this would in itself be something for the younger ones to aim at, a sort of badge of young adulthood. As their names were called they walked up to the stage and took their seats with commendable gravity.

Miss Joseph then gave a short address. She said that their lessons had all had a particular bias towards the brotherhood of mankind, and that they had been learning through each subject how all mankind was interdependent in spite of geographical location and differences in colour, races and creeds. Then she called on Potter.

Potter went on to speak of the work they had done on weights and measures; of the relationship between the kilogramme and the pound, the metre and the foot. He said that throughout the world one or other of those two methods was either in use or understood, and that it was a symbol of the greater understanding which was being accomplished between peoples.

Sapiano spoke of the study the class had made of pests, especially black rot on wheat, boll weevil on cotton, and the Colorado beetle on potatoes. He showed how many countries had pooled their knowledge and results of research on the behaviour, breeding habits and migration of these pests, and were gradually reducing the threat they represented to these important products.

Miss Pegg and Jackson divided the report on Geography between them. Jackson spoke first on the distribution of mineral deposits and vegetable produce over the earth's surface, how a country rich in one was often deficient in the other; and of the interchange and interdependence which inevitably followed. Miss Pegg dealt with human relationships, stressing the problems facing the post-war world for feeding, clothing and housing its populations. She also made a reference to the thousands of refugees, stateless and unwanted; and to the efforts and programmes of U.N.I.C.E.F.

Fernman as usual had a trump card up his sleeve. When called he made a signal to someone off-stage, and Welsh and Alison appeared bearing a skeleton between them, together with a sort of gallows. When this arrangement had been set up there was the skeleton hanging from a hook screwed into the top of its skull, gently revolving at the end of a cord. This was somewhat in the nature of comic relief, and the school showed its approval by laughing uproariously. But levity soon evaporated when Fernman began to speak; his voice was clear and precise and he had a strong sense of the dramatic. Calmly he told them that it was a female skeleton; that was a fact and could easily be proved. But he could not say with any assurance whether she had been Chinese or French or German or Greek; nor could he say if she had been brown or white or a mixture of both. And from that, he said, the class had concluded that basically all people were the same; the trimmings might be different but the foundations were all laid out according to the same blue-print. Fernman was wonderful; he had them eating out of his hand.

Miss Dare's contribution was something of an anti-climax after Fernman's performance, and she seemed to realise it. She spoke about the problems which all humanity has to face in terms of sickness and disease, and of the advantages gained by interchange of knowledge, advice and assistance.

Miss Dodd reported on the period of History the class had studied – the Reformation in England. She told of the struggles of men of independent spirit against clerical domination and of their efforts to break from established religious traditions. From those early beginnings gradually grew the idea of tolerance for the beliefs and cultures of others, and the now common interest in trying to study and understand those cultures.

Denham's report was a bit of a shock. He severely criticised the general pattern of P.T. and games, emphasising the serious limitations of space obtaining and the effect of that limitation on their games activities. He complained that the P.T. was ill-conceived and pointless, and the routine monotonous; he could see no advantage in doing it; a jolly good game was far better. Apparently he was voicing the opinions of all the boys, for they cheered him loudly.

When the reports were over, Denham called two children at random from the audience and asked them to write the name of each teacher, including the Head on a slip of paper. These slips were folded and placed in a hat, juggled vigorously, and then withdrawn one by one. The names were called:

Mr Weston
Mrs Dale-Evans
Miss Phillips

Denham and Miss Joseph led the others off the stage and the teachers took their seats, Weston big and bushily untidy between the two women. Then the questioning began.

I believe I would have gone a long way to see what followed; it was an experience which I shall not easily forget.

The questions were mostly from the two top classes, probably because the young children were either too timid or too uninformed to formulate their questions. The teachers had no briefing, and were often caught out stammering in their indecision. But here again, I received a big surprise. The frilly, seemingly brainless Miss Euphemia Phillips proved to be the coolest and best informed of the three. She dealt with questions put to her with candour and authority, and would often intervene skilfully to assist one of the others without causing embarrassment.

Weston cut a very ridiculous figure. In the face of Denham's blunt criticisms and Fernman's adroit questioning, he found himself completely nonplussed and tried to bluster his way out with a show of offended dignity. He could not effectively support the P.T. exercises, for which he was partly responsible, as having any definite physical advantage. Denham was a trained boxer, and insisted that such exercises were only advantageous if practised daily and for more sustained periods; P.T. twice weekly for twenty minutes was a waste of time, he asserted.

Once again Miss Phillips took the reins and her stock promptly shot up a hundredfold. She reminded the school that every subject, including P.T. and games, had been carefully considered and fitted into the teaching timetable so that each student received maximum benefit from it. The school with its limited facilities must be considered in terms of the greatest good for the greatest number, and it would be beyond anyone's powers to please everybody.

'Some of you,' she concluded, fixing Denham with innocent eyes, 'are fortunate in your own fine physical development and do not really need the few meagre helpings of P.T. and games which this school can offer; try to remember that there are others for whom our programme is ideally suited. It may be that some of you older boys might even be able to help in that respect.'

Denham was not to be put off by these sugary remarks, and rose in reply.

'Then why do we have to do P.T.? Why don't they take only the kids who need it? The rest of us can have a game of football or something, 'stead of doing a lot of daft things that's no good to us!'

This was a poser, but she came right back at him, her baby-blue eyes twinkling in her delight at this crossing of staves.

'Let's say it is as much an exercise of the mind as it is of the body, Denham. The whole timetable in this school is meant to help you in the world after you leave here, and doing what you are told in spite of not liking it, is part of the training. I feel sure that you will see the point in that.'

That stopped him. Poor Denham knew that he'd been outwitted but he could do nothing about it and sat looking rather rueful, while Miss Phillips' smile broadened; this frilly, innocent-looking puss had gobbled her canary without leaving the tiniest feather. I began to understand how it was that so slight a creature could cope so effectively with her class.

Soon after this, as the morning ended, the Head went on to the stage and closed the proceedings, expressing his pride in all the children and his deep appreciation of their efforts.

CHAPTER 18

THURSDAY, NOVEMBER 18TH was Gillian's birthday. On the Monday evening I had been to Foyle's and bought her a book of poems; it was in my briefcase and I planned to give it to her at lunchtime on her birthday. During mid-morning recess on Tuesday she came into my classroom, where I was, as usual, surrounded by a group of chattering youngsters; on seeing her I excused myself from them and greeted her.

'May I see you for a moment, Mr Braithwaite?' Most of the youngsters' inquisitive ears were obviously tuned in to her remarks.

'Certainly, Miss Blanchard.' We walked to the rear of the class out of earshot of the smiling, whispering group.

'Got a surprise for you.'

'Oh, yes? What is it?'

'Thursday is my birthday.'

'No surprise, I already knew.'

'I've ordered dinner for two at the "Poisson d'Or". Special, with wine.'

'Sounds good. Where's the "Poisson d'Or"?'

'It's a new place in Chelsea. Supposed to be very good; you know – *très élégant*.'

'Good, I'm fond of *très élégant*.'

'That's fine then. We can see *Paisan* at the Academy and dine afterwards.'

'Right, it's a date.' Smiling, she hurried out.

I walked back to the group of children and into a barrage of questions. It was the first time they had seen her in our classroom and their quick minds were full of meanings and speculations.

'Is Miss Blanchard your girlfriend?' Tich Jackson queried. 'She's smashing, isn't she?'

By agreeing that Miss Blanchard was smashing I managed to parry the first part of the question. The girls began to discuss Gillian's hair, clothes and shoes, and the conversation was steered into smoother water. Pamela said nothing; I had the feeling she did not share their enthusiasm for Gillian.

When Thursday came I felt as excited as a sandboy, and it was with a feeling of relief that I heard the final bell at 4.30 p.m.

Gillian looked very lovely in an ensemble of light grey with a ridiculous little black hat perched saucily on her head. Weston followed us through the gates, and I thought to myself: 'I'm damned sure he wishes he were me.' We caught a bus and changed to another at Aldgate, where we sat in front on the upper deck. Gillian immediately linked her arm in mine and we were together in a private, wonderful world of pleasant, whispered, unimportant talk about anything and everything which caught our attention en route. We would play a game of our own invention which we called post-chaise. For this purpose the bus was a stagecoach, and each stop a staging post or inn; we took turns at thinking up appropriate names for the stops, befitting their surroundings. For instance, the Aldgate stop was 'Ye Pump and Bells' after Aldgate Pump and the nearby church tower; the next stop around the turn into Leadenhall Street was 'Ye Axe and Virgin', and so on. The one who failed to produce a reasonably good name would be debited with a point. Points were valued at fifty a penny. It was great fun, and we rocked with laughter at our own attempts at improvisation.

The film was wonderful and we left the cinema somewhat subdued by the artistry and sheer reality of it, and walked through Piccadilly Circus to catch a bus for Chelsea.

The 'Poisson d'Or' was, as Gillian had said, *très élégant*. It was one of those smart little restaurants that win a reputation and a following overnight, and then as quickly lose it. On every table, in place of flowers, was a live goldfish in a small glass bowl. The walls were decorated to depict a fish's world of waving weed and coralline forms, and the indirect lighting was cleverly manipulated to produce an effect of underwater movement. I felt sure that a meal here would be an expensive affair.

The *maître d'hôtel* came forward and directed us to our table, with a questioning glance at me. We sat down and chatted quietly, both of us very much aware of the special something between us, recognised, but waiting to be acknowledged. Eventually we both realised that the service was being exceptionally slow, especially to our table, for other diners seemed to have waiters hovering around them all the time.

Presently a waiter brought us a bill of fare which he placed on the table, and departed. Annoyance was large in Gillian's eyes, but I took it up and we spent a little time carefully choosing the food. The waiter returned and took our order, his manner casual with an implied discourtesy, and he was so long returning that I became really uneasy and annoyed. What was the fellow playing at?

He came at last with the soup. Whether by accident or design, some of the soup was spilled from my plate on to the cloth. I sat back expecting that he would do something about it as good service demanded, but he merely stood there looking at me, with a faint sneer on his face. Gillian reacted suddenly. With a swift movement she gathered up her gloves and handbag. 'Let's go, Rick.'

Head high, she walked ahead of me towards the doorway through a gauntlet of enquiring eyes. I collected my coat from the cloakroom and quickly joined her.

Outside she turned to me, her eyes like coals in her pale face. 'Will you take me home, please?'

I signalled a passing taxi. Inside the taxi she sat as far away from me as the seat would allow, as cold and distant as any stranger, her face averted to gaze unseeing at the passing scene. I felt suddenly let down and wished I were far away from her and the school and everything.

What had I done? Was the waiter's stupid discourtesy to be blamed on me? She had chosen the place, yet at the first sign of bother she had turned on me. Was that all that our friendship meant to her? The taxi stopped at her direction outside a block of flats in a quiet street near the embankment. She got out and hesitated while I paid the driver, then turned and ran up the steps. I watched her, expecting that she would disappear forever inside, but she turned and said:

'Aren't you coming?' in a tight, angry voice. This Gillian was a stranger, a cold, hateful stranger. I was tempted to hurry away from her, but she meant too much to me. I'd see it through, whatever it was. I followed her inside.

Her flat was on the ground floor. We entered a room which was small but comfortably furnished with deep chairs and an old-fashioned overstuffed sofa. Three low bookcases were ranged round the room, their tops laden with an array of bric-à-brac, bits and pieces of ornamental pottery and brasswork, silverware and glass. The carpet was deep-piled and on the walls were a few prints by modern impressionist painters. Three doors led off from this room. I guessed to bedroom, kitchenette and bathroom. Everything here was in harmony except ourselves.

Gillian threw hat, handbag and gloves on to the sofa with an impatient gesture and invited me to sit, then began to move about the room idly fixing and straightening the things on top of the bookcases. Her actions were jerky and hurried, as if she were unsuccessfully trying to control some high-powered dynamo inside her. My eyes followed her every movement; I was tense waiting for the outburst which I was sure would come. At last with a few quick strides she pushed open one of the doors and was gone.

I took the book of poems from my briefcase and laid it on a low coffee table; the whole evening was irretrievably spoilt, and this was certainly not the time to present my gift as I had planned.

In a few moments she returned, apparently calmer. She was about to sit down when she saw the little package; she picked it up, tore off the wrappings, and looked at it. Then her hands dropped by her side in an attitude of despair.

'Damn you, damn you.' Each word was torn out of her like a dry, painful cough. 'Why did you just sit there and take it?'

'I suppose you're referring to the waiter.'

'Yes, why did you?'

'What was I supposed to do, hit him? Did you want a scene in that place?'

'Yes, I wanted a scene. I wanted a big, bloody awful scene.' The words sounded foul coming from her. She was glaring at me, her body bent forward at the waist, her arms raised slightly backwards, like an agitated bird.

'What good would that have done?'

'I don't know and I don't care. I wanted you to hit him, to beat him, down, down . . .' She was nearly incoherent with anger and sobbing.

'It wouldn't help, it never helps.'

'Why not? Just who do you think you are, Jesus Christ? Sitting there all good and patient? Or were you afraid? Is that it? Were you afraid of that damned little waiter, that bloody little peasant of a waiter?'

'You're being hysterical, Gillian; beating people up never solves anything.'

'Doesn't it? Well, you tell me what does. You've been taking it and taking it, don't you think it's time you showed a little spirit?' She was becoming quite shrill now, like a fishwife.

'Someone else always has to fight for you, to take your part. Clinty stood up for you against Weston; the Dare girl stood up for you on the train; was I supposed to stand up for you tonight?'

I felt tired, awfully tired of the whole thing.

'Let's not talk any more about it.'

'That's right, run away from it.'

'Oh, let's forget it.'

'Forget it? Do you know what today is? I'd planned and planned for it to be nice and wonderful for us. Today of all days. I could have gone somewhere else or done something else, but no, I had to be with you, and you calmly tell me to forget it. Oh I hate you, I hate you, you damn black. . . .'

With a scream she hurled the book at me and followed behind it, her hands stiff and clawing, like a demented creature. So forceful was her attack that I was nearly knocked off balance, but I grabbed her roughly, pinioning her arms, keeping her long nails away from my face. Hers was the strength of violent anger; for a while she struggled, silently and fiercely; then abruptly she went limp and leaned against me, moaning with her face against my coat.

When I felt sure that I could safely release her, I led her to a chair and she sat sideways, crying softly. I sat nearby, nervously watching her, knowing in my heart that this was the end; knowing that I ought to leave her now, but loath to go, drawing the moment out as far as I could. Presently she turned to me and asked:

'What are we going to do, Rick?'

'I don't know, Gillian.' What could I say? There was a small flutter of hope in my heart and I held my breath, waiting for her next words.

'Is that the sort of thing we'd be faced with, all the time?'

She was speaking about us, both of us.

'Do you mean the waiter thing?'

'Yes, does it happen to you often?'

'Not often, hardly ever really. You see, it never happened to me while I was in the R.A.F., and since becoming a civilian I have not been anywhere socially until, well, until we started going out together.'

I sat watching her, uncertain what to say. She had been hurt, humiliated by the waiter's uncouth behaviour, but had she not known or heard of that sort of thing before? She was English, and had spent all her life in England; was she truly free from the virus of racial intolerance?

'Didn't you know that such things happened?' I asked.

'Not really. I have heard and read about it in a vague sort of way, but I had never imagined it happening to me.'

'It wouldn't have if you hadn't been with me.'

She looked up quickly, the hurt still strong in her dark eyes.

'What does that mean, Rick?'

'It need never happen to you again.' In spite of myself, in

spite of the love tearing at my inside, I was saying these things, not wanting to, but saying them.

'Is that what you want, Rick?'

I could not answer her. The whole thing was suddenly too big for me, too involved, too mixed-up with other people, millions of other people whom I did not know, would never know, but who were capable of hating me on sight because of her; not because she was beautiful and good and cultured and lovable, but merely because she was white.

'No, Gillian, that's not what I want.'

My mind was seeing the dangers and the difficulties, but my heart was answering boldly and carelessly. She rose and came over to sit on the arm of my chair.

'I love you, Rick.'

'I love you, Gillian.'

'But I'm afraid, Rick, terribly afraid now. Everything seemed all right before, but now it's all a bit frightening. How do you take it so calmly, Rick, don't you mind about it?'

'Mind? Oh yes, I do mind, but I'm learning how to mind and still live. At first it was terrible, but gradually I'm learning what it means to live with dignity inside my black skin.'

And then I told her about my life in Britain, the whole thing, everything which led to my becoming a teacher and meeting her. She listened quietly, not interrupting, but soon, somehow, her hand was in mine, its firm, gentle pressure supporting, comforting, uplifting.

'I'm sorry, Rick,' she murmured when I had finished.

'Don't be sorry about it, my dear. I just thought I should let you know the sort of thing which happened and is probably still likely to happen.'

'Oh, not about that, about the things I said to you tonight.'

'I understand; it is forgiven – it was nothing.'

For a while we sat united in our thoughts, needing no words, no further reassurance. Then she squeezed my hand and said, smiling:

'I'll write to Mummy tomorrow. I've told her so much about you she won't be surprised.'

'Won't she mind?'

'I suppose she will, but she's very understanding really. We talked about it last time I was at home.'

'And your father?'

'Mother will get to work on him I expect. Anyway I'll write and say you'll be down with me next weekend. I think you'll like them, Rick; they're awfully sweet, really.'

I stared through the window into the night. Life followed no pattern, no planned course. Before tonight I had not even kissed this sweet, beloved girl, yet now, for good or ill, the die was cast.

'Rick.'

'Yes?'

'I'm not very brave really, you know, about what people will say and things like that, but I do love you so completely, I'll try to be good for you. I think we can be happy together Rick.'

'We'll try.'

She was crying again, very softly. I held her close, wanting to protect her forever, from everything. I was afraid, not for myself, but for this sweet person who was so unhesitatingly prepared to link her life with mine. But others had met this problem before and had succeeded in rising above it. God willing, I'd try to do the same. We'd both try.

CHAPTER 19

THE SCHOOL SEEMED to be the touchstone of my happiness. Since joining it I had experienced a new assurance and strength, and gradually I was acquiring a real understanding, not only of the youngsters in my charge but also of the neighbourhood and its people. Sometimes I would walk through Watney Street, that short dingy thoroughfare of small shops lined on both sides with barrows of every description: fruit barrows, fish barrows, groceries, vegetables, sweets, haberdashery. Some of the barrows were really mobile extensions of the shops in front of which they stood, and served as display counters for the curious confusion of assorted goods which left little or no room for customers inside the shop.

The vendors soon knew who I was, and would smile pleasantly as I passed. Sometimes I would hear one say to another: 'That's our Marie's teacher.' Or, 'He's teaching at Greenslade School. Our Joanie's in his class, he's ever so nice.'

Once I stopped at a fruit barrow. The large woman in bright apron and wellington boots smiled as she weighed the apples.

'Our Maur's got engaged last Sunday.' I knew that I was expected to know who 'our Maur' was, but my glance must have betrayed my mystification.

'You know, Ann Blore in your class, Maur's her older sister; got engaged to an American soldier, ever such a nice boy.'

Another time it was: 'Our Jacqueline won't be in today, been up all night with her stomach. Her gran's taking her to the doctor's today. I sorta hoped you'd come this way so I could tell you.'

147

That one was easy. There was only one Jacqueline in my class.

Often I would stop and chat with these folks who were always eager to show their friendly acceptance of me, by drawing me into things concerning their children and themselves as though they believed I had a right to know.

Occasionally their conversation caused me some embarrassment, as when the stout Jewish fruit vendor, Mrs Joseph, seeing me at the end of the queue waiting to purchase apples from her, calmly called me to the front and weighed and packaged my order, explaining to the frowning customers that I was 'her Moir's' teacher and was probably in a hurry.

There was growing up between the children and myself a real affection which I found very pleasant and encouraging. Each day I tried to present to them new facts in a way which would excite and stimulate their interest, and gradually they were developing a readiness to comment and also a willingness to tolerate the expressed opinions of others, even when those opinions were diametrically opposed to theirs. At first these differences of opinion set tempers alight, and the children were apt to resort to the familiar expletives when they found themselves bested by more persuasive or logical colleagues. Whenever this happened I deliberately ignored it, and gradually the attitude of the majority of the class to strong language proved sufficient to discourage its too liberal use.

I was learning from them as well as teaching them. I learned to see them in relation to their surroundings, and in that way to understand them. At first I had been rather critical of their clothing, and thought their tight sweaters, narrow skirts and jeans unsuitable for school wear, but now that they were taking greater interest in personal tidiness, I could understand that such clothes merely reflected vigorous personalities in a relentless search for self-expression.

Just about this time a new supply teacher, Mr Bell, was sent to our school as supernumerary to the Staff for a few weeks. He was about forty years old, a tall, wiry, man who had had some experience with the Army Education Service. It was arranged that he should act as relief teacher for some lessons, including two periods of P.T. with the senior boys. One of Mr Bell's hobbies was fencing: he was something of a perfectionist and impatient of anyone whose co-ordination was not as smooth and controlled as his own. He would repeat a P.T. movement or exercise over and over again until it was executed with clockwise precision, and though the boys grumbled against his discipline they seemed eager to prove to him that they were quite capable of doing any exercise he could devise, and with a skill that very nearly matched his own.

This was especially true in the cases of Ingham, Fernman and Seales, who would always place themselves at the head of the line as an example and encouragement to the others. The least athletic of these was Richard Buckley, a short, fat boy, amiable and rather dim, who could read and write after a fashion, and could never be provoked to any semblance of anger or heat. He was pleasant and jolly and a favourite with the others, who, though they themselves chivvied him unmercifully, were ever ready in his defence against outsiders.

Buckley was no good at P.T. or games; he just was not built for such pursuits. Yet, such is the perversity of human nature, he strenuously resisted any efforts to leave him out or overlook him when games were being arranged. His attempts at accomplishing such simple gymnastic performances as the 'forward roll' and 'star jump' reduced the rest of the P.T. class to helpless hilarity, but he persisted with a singleness of purpose, which though unproductive, was nothing short of heroic.

Buckley was Bell's special whipping boy. Fully aware of the lad's physical limitations, he would encourage him to try other and more difficult exercises, with apparently the sole purpose of obtaining some amusement from the pitiably ridiculous results. Sometimes the rest of the class would protest; and then Bell would turn on them the full flood of his invective. The boys mentioned this in their 'Weekly Review', and Mr Florian decided to discuss it at a Staff Meeting.

'The boys seem to be a bit bothered by remarks you make to them during P.T., Mr Bell.'

'To which remarks do you refer, Mr Florian?' Bell never used the term 'Sir', seeming to think it 'infra dig'. Even when he granted him the 'Mr Florian' he gave to this form of address the suggestion of a sneer.

'From their review it would seem that you are unnecessarily critical of their persons.'

'Do you mean their smell?'

'Well, yes, that and the state of their clothing.'

'I've advised them to wash.'

'These are the words which appear in one review.' The Headmaster produced a notebook, Fernman's, and read: '"Some of you stink like old garbage."'

His tone was cool, detached, judicial.

'I was referring to their feet. Many of them never seem to wash their feet, and when they take their shoes off the stink is dreadful.'

'Many of them live in homes where there are very few facilities for washing, Mr Bell.'

'Surely enough water is available for washing their feet if they really wanted to.'

'Then they'd put on the same smelly socks and shoes to which you also object.'

'I've got to be in contact with them and it isn't very pleasant.'

'Have you ever lived in this area, Mr Bell?'

'No fear.'

'Then you know nothing about the conditions prevailing. The water you so casually speak of is more often to be found in the walls and on the floors than in the convenient wash basin or bath to which you are accustomed. I've visited homes of some of these children where water for a family in an upstairs flat had to be fetched by bucket or pail from the single back-yard tap which served five or six families. You may see, therefore, that so elementary a function as washing the feet might present many difficulties.'

Bell was silent at this.

'I've no wish to interfere, or tell you how to do your work; you're an experienced teacher and know more about P.T. than I'll ever do,' – the Old Man was again patient, encouraging – 'but try to be a little more understanding about their difficulties.' He then turned to other matters, but it was clear that Bell was considerably put out by the rebuke.

Matters came to a head that Monday afternoon. I was not present in the gym, but was able to reconstruct the sequence of events with reasonable accuracy from the boys' reports and Bell's subsequent admissions.

During the P.T. session he had been putting them through their paces in the 'astride vault' over the buck, all except Buckley, who was somewhat under the weather and wisely stood down from attempting the rather difficult jump, but without reference to or permission from Bell, who was not long in discovering the absence of his favourite diversion.

'Buckley,' he roared.

'Yes, Sir.'

'Come on, boy, I'm waiting.' He was standing in his usual position beside the buck in readiness to arrest the fall of any lad who might be thrown off balance by an awkward approach or incorrect execution of the movement. But the boy did not move, and the master stared at him amazed and angry at this unexpected show of defiance by the one generally considered to be most timid and tractable in the whole class.

'Fatty can't do it, Sir, it's too high for him,' Denham interposed.

'Shut up, Denham,' Bell roared. 'If I want your opinion I will ask for it.' He left his station by the buck and walked to where Buckley was standing. The boy watched his threatening approach, fear apparent in his eyes.

'Well, Buckley,' Bell towered over the unhappy youth, 'are you going to do as you're told?'

'Yes, Sir.' Buckley's capitulation was as sudden as his refusal.

The others stopped to watch as he stood looking at the buck, licking his lips nervously while waiting for the instructor to resume his position. It may have been fear or determination or a combination of both, but Buckley launched himself at the buck in furious assault, and in spite of Bell's restraining arms, boy and buck crashed on the floor with a sickening sound as one leg of the buck snapped off with the sound of a pistol shot. The class stood in shocked silence watching Buckley, who remained as he fell, inert and pale; then they rushed to his assistance. All except Potter; big, good-natured Potter seemed to have lost his reason. He snatched up the broken metal-bound leg and advanced on Bell, screaming:

'You bloody bastard, you f—ing bloody bastard.'

'Put that thing down, Potter, don't be a fool,' Bell spluttered, backing away from the hysterical boy.

'You made him do it; he didn't want to and you made him,' Potter yelled.

'Don't be a fool, Potter, put it down,' Bell appealed.

'I'll do you in, you bloody murderer.' Bell was big, but in his anger Potter seemed bigger, his improvised club a fearsome extension of his thick forearm.

That was where I rushed in. Tich Jackson, frightened by the sight of Buckley, limp and white on the floor, and the enraged Potter, slobbering at the instructor in murderous fury, had dashed upstairs to my classroom shouting: 'Sir, quick, they're fighting in the gym.' I followed his disappearing figure in time to see Bell backed against a wall, with Potter advancing on him.

'Hold it, Potter,' I called. He turned at the sound of my voice and I quickly placed myself between them. 'Let's have that, Potter.' I held out my hand towards the boy, but he stared past me at Bell, whimpering in his emotion. Anger had completely taken hold of him, and he looked very dangerous.

'Come on, Potter,' I repeated, 'hand it over and go lend a hand with Buckley.'

He turned to look towards his prostrate friend and I quickly moved up to him and seized the improvised club; he released it to me without any resistance and went back to join the group around Buckley. Bell then walked away and out of the room, and I went up to the boys. Denham rose and faced me, his face white with rage.

'Potts should have done the bastard like he did Fatty, just 'cos he wouldn't do the bloody jump.'

I let that pass; they were angry and at such times quickly reverted to the old things, the words, the discourtesies. I stooped down beside Buckley, who was now sitting weakly on the floor, supported by Sapiano and Seales, and smiling up at them as if ashamed of himself for having been the cause of so much fuss.

'How do you feel, old man?' I enquired.

'Cor, Sir,' he cried, smiling, 'me tum does hurt.'

'He fell on to the buck. You should have seen 'im, Sir.'

'Gosh, you should've heard the noise when the leg smashed.'

'Mr Bell couldn't catch Fatty, Sir, you should've seen him.'

Most of them were trying to talk all at once, eager to give me all the details.

'Bleeding bully, always picking on Fats.' This from Sapiano, whose volatile Maltese temperament was inclined to flare up very easily.

'If I'd had the wood I'd have done the f—er in and no bleeding body would have stopped me.' Denham was aching for trouble and didn't care who knew it. Bell had slipped away unharmed after hurting his friend, and Denham wanted a substitute. But I would not look at him, or even hear the things he said. Besides, I liked Denham; in spite of his rough manner and speech he was an honest, dependable person with a strong sense of independence.

'Can you stand up, Buckley?'

With some assistance from Seales and Sapiano the boy got to his feet; he looked very pale and unsteady. I turned to Denham: 'Will you help the others to take Buckley up to Mrs Dale-Evans and ask her to give him some sweet tea; leave him there and I'll meet you all in the classroom in a few minutes.'

Without waiting for his reply I hurried off to the staffroom in search of Bell.

I was in something of a quandary. I knew that it was quite possible Buckley was all right, but there was no knowing whether he had sustained any internal injury not yet apparent. The Council's rules required that all accidents be reported and logged; the Headmaster should be informed forthwith, and in the light of what he had said to Bell so very recently, there would most certainly be a row.

I went up to the staffroom and found Bell washing his face at the sink.

'I've sent Buckley upstairs for a cup of tea,' I said. 'I suppose he'll be all right, anyway he was walking under his own steam.'

'What happens now?' His voice was querulous.

'You should know as well as I do,' I replied. 'Shouldn't you see the Old Man and make some kind of report?'

'Yes, I suppose I'd better get over to his office right away. I should have attended to the Buckley boy, but the other one rushed me. Thanks for helping out.'

'Oh, that's all right,' I replied. 'But why did you insist on the boy doing the vault?'

'I had to, don't you see; he just stood there refusing to obey and the others were watching me; I just had to do something.' His whole attitude now was defensive.

'I'm not criticising you, Mr Bell, just asking. Buckley's a bit of a mascot with the others, you know, and I suppose that is why Potter got out of hand.'

'I guess it was the way he jumped, or something, but I couldn't grab him. He hit the buck too low and sent it flying.'

'He is a bit awkward, isn't he; anyway I'm sure the Old Man will understand how it happened.'

'He might be a bit difficult, especially after what he said the other day.'

'Not necessarily. After all, it was an accident and thank Heaven it's not very serious.'

He dried his hands and moved towards the door. 'I suppose they'll really go to town on this in their Weekly Reviews,' he remarked.

'I'll ask the boys to say nothing about it. I don't suppose Potter is now feeling any too pleased with himself at his conduct.'

As he left Clinty came into the staffroom.

'What's happening, Rick?' she asked. 'I just saw some of your boys taking Fatty Buckley upstairs. What's happened to him?'

I told her about the incident and added: 'Bell has just gone to the Old Man's office to report the matter.'

'Well, what do you know?' she chuckled. 'Fancy Potter going for Bell like that. I always thought that boy a bit of a softie, but you never know with those quiet ones, do you?'

'He was not the only one. Sapiano and Denham were just as wild, I think, but they were too busy fussing over Buckley to bother with Bell.'

'He is a bit of a tyro, isn't he. This might make him take it a bit easier.'

'I don't think the boys mind his being strict during P.T. It's just that Buckley's a bit of a fool and they resented his being hurt. If it had been Denham or someone like that, I'm sure they would have done nothing.'

'Yes, I guess you're right. Bell is a good teacher. I wonder how long the Divisional Office will let him stay here. I hope he hasn't had too much of a fright.'

'Oh, he'll get over that. Now I must go and have a word with my boys.'

I left her. For some inexplicable reason I felt nervous about being alone with Clinty; I felt that there was something she wanted to say to me, and for my part I did not want to hear it.

In the classroom the boys were sitting closely grouped together, looking rather sheepish. I knew they were feeling aggrieved and, according to their lights, justifiably so; but nevertheless the matter of Potter's behaviour had to be dealt with.

'How's Buckley?' I asked.

'We left him upstairs with Mrs Dale-Evans, Sir. He didn't want to stay, he kept saying he was all right. But she told him if he wasn't quiet she'd give him some castor-oil, Sir. Ugh!' They all managed a smile at Seale's remark.

'Good,' I replied, 'I expect he'll be quite all right. But there is something I want to say to you about this unfortunate incident.' I sat down on the edge of Fernman's desk.

'Potter, there is nothing I can think of which can excuse your shocking conduct in the gym.'

Potter's mouth fell open; he looked at me in surprise, gulped a few times and stammered:

'But it was him, Sir, Mr Bell, making Fatty fall and that.' His voice was shrill with outrage at my remark.

'Mr Bell was the master there, Potter, and anything that happened in the gym was his responsibility. Buckley's mishap was no excuse for you to make such an attack on your teacher.'

'But Fatty told him he couldn't do it, Sir, and he made him, he made him, Sir.'

Potter was very near tears. His distress was greater because of what he believed was the further injustice of my censure. The others, too, were looking at me with the same expression.

'That may be, Potter. I am not now concerned with Mr Bell's conduct, but with yours. You came very near to getting yourself into very serious trouble because you were unable to control your temper. Not only was your language foul and disgusting, but you armed yourself with a weapon big enough and heavy enough to cause very serious harm. What do you think would have happened if everyone had behaved like you and had all turned on Mr Bell like a pack of mad wolves?' I waited for this to sink in a bit, but Potter interjected:

'I thought he had done Fatty in, Sir, he looked all huddled up like, Sir.'

'I see. So you didn't wait to find out but rushed in with your club like a hoodlum to smash and kill, is that it? Your friend was hurt and you wanted to hurt back; suppose instead of a piece of wood it had been a knife, or a gun, what then?' Potter was pale, and he was not the only one.

'Potts didn't think. He was narked, we was all narked, seeing Fatty on the deck. I wasn't half bleeding wild myself.'

'You're missing the point, Denham. I think you're all missing the point. We sit in this classroom day after day and talk of things, and you all know what's expected of you; but at the first sign of bother you forget it all. In two weeks you'll all be at work and lots of things will happen which will annoy you, make you wild. Are you going to resort to clubs and knives every time you're upset or angered?' I stood up. 'You'll meet foremen or supervisors or workmates who'll do things to upset you, sometimes deliberately. What then, Denham? What about that, Potter? Your Headmaster is under fire from many quarters because he believes in you – because he really believes that by the time you leave here you will have learned to exercise a little self-control at the times when it is most needed. His success or failure will be reflected in the way you conduct yourselves after you leave him. If today's effort is an example of your future behaviour I hold out very little hope for you.'

At this moment Buckley walked in, smiling broadly and seemingly none the worse for wear. I waited until he was seated then went on:

'I've no wish to belabour this matter, but it cannot be left like this. Potter, you were very discourteous to your P.T. instructor, and it is my opinion that you owe him an apology.'

Potter stared at me, his mouth open in amazement at my remark; but before he could speak Denham leapt to his feet.

'Apologise?' His voice was loud in anger. 'Why should Potts apologise? He didn't do him any harm. Why should he apologise to him just because he's a bleeding teacher?' He stood there, legs slightly apart, heavy-shouldered and truculent, glaring at me. The others were watching us, but agreeing with him; I could feel their resentment hardening.

'Please sit down Denham, and remember that in this class we are always able to discuss things, no matter how difficult or unpleasant, without shouting at each other.'

I waited, fearful of this unexpected threat to our pleasant relationship; he looked around at his colleagues indecisively, then abruptly sat down. I continued, in a very friendly tone:

'That was a fair question, Denham, although you will agree it was put a little, shall we say, indelicately?'

I smiled as I said this, and, in spite of his anger, Denham smiled briefly too. I went on:

'Potter, are you quite pleased and satisfied with the way you behaved to your P.T. teacher?'

Potter looked at me for a moment, then murmured, 'No, Sir.'

'But he couldn't help it,' Denham interjected.

'That may be so, Denham, but Potter agrees that his own actions were unsatisfactory; upon reflection he himself is not pleased with what he did.'

E.R. BRAITHWAITE

'How's about Mr Bell then: how's about him apologising to Buckley?' Denham was not to be dissuaded from his attitude.

'Yes, how about him?' echoed Sapiano.

'My business is with you, not with Mr Bell,' I replied.

This was not going to be easy, I thought. Denham was getting a bit nasty; the usual 'Sir' had disappeared from his remarks, and Sapiano was following suit.

'It's easy for you to talk, Sir, nobody tries to push you around.' Seales' voice was clear and calm, and the others turned to took at him, to support him. His statement touched something deep inside of me, something which had been dormant for months, but now awoke to quick, painful remembering. Without realising what I was doing I got up and walked to where he sat and stood beside his desk.

'I've been pushed around, Seales,' I said quietly, 'in a way I cannot explain to you. I've been pushed around until I began to hate people so much that I wanted to hurt them, really hurt them. I know how it feels, believe me, and one thing I learned, Seales, is to try always to be a bit bigger than the people who hurt me. It is easy to reach for a knife or a gun; but then you become merely a tool and the knife or gun takes over, thereby creating new and bigger problems without solving a thing. So what happens when there is no weapon handy?'

I felt suddenly annoyed with myself for giving way to my emotion, and abruptly walked back to my desk. The class seemed to feel that something had touched me deeply and were immediately sympathetic in their manner.

'The point I want to make, Potter,' I continued, 'is whether you are really growing up and learning to stand squarely on your own feet. When you begin work at Covent Garden you might someday have cause to be very angry; what will you do then? The whole idea of this school is to teach you to discipline yourself. In this instance you lost your temper and behaved badly to your teacher. Do you think you are big enough to make an apology to him?'

Potter fidgeted in his seat and looked uncertainly at me, then replied: 'Yes, Sir.'

'It's always difficult to apologise, Potter, especially to

someone you feel justified in disliking. But remember that you are not doing it for Mr Bell's sake, but your own.'

I sat down. They were silent, but I realised that they understood what I meant. Potter stood up:

'Is he in the staffroom, Sir?'

'I think he should be there now, Potter.'

Denham and Seales stood and joined Potter and together they went to find Bell. I called Buckley.

'How are you feeling, Buckley?'

'Okay, Sir,' he replied, as jovial as ever.

'What will your parents say about all this, Buckley?' I was being devious, but, I thought, necessarily so.

'I shan't tell 'em, Sir. Must I, Sir?'

'It's up to you, Buckley. If you feel fine there's no need to bother; but if in the next few days or weeks you feel any pain, it would be best to mention it so that they'd know what to do.'

In a few minutes the boys were back, Potter looking red and embarrassed; behind them came Mr Bell.

'May I speak to your boys for a moment, Mr Braithwaite?' He came and stood beside my desk and I nodded to him.

'I want to say to all of you,' he began, 'that I'm sorry about what happened in the gym a little while ago. I think that one way or another we were all a bit silly, but the sooner we forget the whole thing, the better.'

'How're you feeling now, boy?' He addressed himself to Buckley.

'Okay, Sir,' the boy replied.

'Fine. Well. I suppose we'll see each other as usual next week.' And with that he was gone, having made as friendly a gesture as his evident nervousness would allow.

The boys seemed not unwilling to let the matter drop, so we turned our attention to the discussion of other things.

CHAPTER 20

LATER THAT WEEK the school was invaded by a newspaper. The Headmaster had obtained the necessary L.C.C. permission for such a visit, having been persuaded that he could present his views and policy to a much wider public through this medium, and that it was an excellent opportunity to reply to his critics and detractors. The day before the reporters arrived he called a staff meeting to inform us of their visit and to ask for our cooperation. From his enthusiastic remarks it seemed undoubtedly a sound idea, and we all agreed to help. It was decided to say nothing beforehand to the children, as the plan was to photograph them at their normal pursuits.

They arrived about ten o'clock in the morning, a reporter and two cameramen. Soon they were everywhere, their shutters snapping and bulbs flashing unexpectedly and disturbingly. The children became somewhat excited, and the members of my class were constantly craning their necks towards the door in the hope of having their pictures 'took'. During the morning the Head sent for me and introduced me to the reporter and cameramen, who were having a cup of tea with him in his room.

'Mr Braithwaite, these gentlemen would like to speak with you for a moment.' I sat down and the reporter began.

'When the Headmaster told us that you were on his staff, I thought it would be a good idea to have some special photographs of you with your class; you know, as an example of the spirit of democracy and tolerance in the school.'

I studied him for a few moments. Democracy and tolerance, how glibly these people used those words! Suddenly I didn't like it and exclaimed involuntarily:

'Why, what purpose would that serve?'

'Well, at least it would show that in Britain there is no colour bar.'

'I'm sorry,' I said, bored by this travesty of the truth. 'Look here, I am at this school as a teacher, that and nothing more; the Council did not employ me because I am coloured, and I have no wish to be used as propaganda for any idea or scheme, especially the one you just mentioned.'

I spoke with some heat, I suppose, for they all looked at me in surprise. The Head turned to me:

'I must confess to being the one who initiated the idea, Mr Braithwaite, believing that any publicity given to your presence on the staff would benefit the school. I do not think there are many Negro teachers in England, and we are fortunate to have you and would like to say so publicly.'

'I'm sorry, Mr Florian,' I replied, 'but I am not really concerned with the public view of my presence here, and I have no wish to be a sop to public conscience on matters of tolerance. I am merely a teacher and would prefer to remain unpublicised except in circumstances of my own choosing.'

They were disappointed but they left it at that, and soon went on with their business, photographing the children in classrooms, at meals, in the playground, and at the midday dance session. Bell put the boys through their paces before the cameras, he himself stripped down to vest and slacks. The children co-operated magnificently, stimulated by the prospect of that fleeting moment of immortality when they would see themselves in the newspaper, the pride of their parents and friends, and the envy of less fortunate youngsters.

On the following Monday the illustrated report appeared. I call it that for want of a term better descriptive of the malicious outrage which passed for journalism. There were pictures, certainly, but the 'report' was restricted to a few captions and a short paragraph, none of which were truthfully descriptive of the pictures above them. Of the three pictures which appeared one showed Mr Florian as a small, grey, aged figure dancing with one of the girls, in ridiculous contrast to the whirling-skirted youngsters around him, who were made to look sleazy and uncouth; another picture showed some of the children with cigarettes hanging from their mouths and wearing expressions of bored depravity; the third was of the dining hall at dinner time – a thieves' kitchen would have fared better. There was something horribly vulgar about the whole thing which sickened me, and I arrived in school to find the staff very angry at the trick played on them and the school. Mrs Drew told us that the Head wanted to discuss the matter with us during mid-morning recess.

The children were not upset by the publicity; they thought it grand fun, and we discovered that they had been induced to pose with the cigarettes. We all knew that some of them smoked, but the pictures inferred that they smoked openly and together. Any picture would have been acceptable to them, and that day many of them even went far afield to obtain a copy of that newspaper. I suppose the slight increase in circulation effectively soothed any twinge of conscience momentarily experienced by those responsible.

I had never attended so voluble a staff meeting. Each one saw the 'report' as a personal slight on himself or herself. The Old Man was very distressed about the whole thing.

'When I agreed to have the newspaper people here,' he said, 'it was on the understanding that they would report, at some length, on our varied activities here, fairly and objectively. They promised that they would and I believed them. I gave the reporter a carefully prepared summary of our scheme of work to help him in making such a report. Now it seems they have gone out of their way to make us look cheap and ridiculous; they've given more grist to the mill of those who have maligned us without knowing anything about us; they will now be able to point at these photographs and say: "the camera does not lie".' In his agitation he was pulling at his lower lip, an odd habit which appeared in moments of emotional tension. 'I do not know if there is any action open to me against this sort of thing.'

'The whole idea was certainly ill-advised,' remarked Weston pompously, quickly forgetting his own enthusiasm in favour of it.

'I agree, Mr Weston,' the Head said, resignedly. 'It was very ill-advised, and I am entirely to blame.'

'Shut up, Weston,' Clinty cried. 'You were as keen about it as the rest of us.'

'It *is* rather mean of Mr Weston to say that now. At the time all of us were keen on the idea, except perhaps Mr Braithwaite, and he disagreed only on a personal matter.'

'I wonder what happened to all the other pictures they took,' Grace asked. 'I wasted a lot of time getting the girls upstairs into position.'

'Why, it's evident they did not want anything which seemed normal and ordinary. Who wants to read of ordinary children doing ordinary things? They wanted to see spivs and morons and delinquents in their incubator, before their release on an unsuspecting world.'

'What was your objection, Mr Braithwaite?' Miss Phillips asked me.

'Simply that I refused to be paraded as some kind of oddity, that's all.'

'Well, aren't you an oddity? How many black teachers have you met in England?' Weston was right and he knew it.

'As far as I am concerned, Weston, I could only be an oddity to anyone fool enough to imagine or believe that my colour makes me less a man than my white counterpart. I am a teacher and nothing about me is odd or unusual. The reporter gave me the impression that he was more interested in the strangeness of seeing a Negro teacher with white children, and its pictorial appeal to the curious, than in anything I was doing or could do for the children: and on that score, and that alone, I objected.'

'Never mind, Weston,' Clinty teased, 'there's always the *News of the World*. Your turn will come.'

'At least I wasn't made to look ridiculous,' he murmured. We realised he was jabbing at the Old Man.

'No fault of yours, chum,' Clinty replied. 'It's just that you can't dance.' She always had the last word, this irrepressible Cockney.

Now Gillian spoke. Never before had she made any observation during a staff meeting, and usually she treated the general staffroom chatter like the chaff it really was. Now everyone looked at her.

'I have had some little experience with newspapers, and I would like to suggest that you are not in too great a hurry to blame this on the reporter and cameraman; they have no control over what is put into the newspaper. The editor decides what and how much of it is reproduced; and his decisions are largely determined by public taste. This school has, I gather, been often criticised in some quarters, and it must be very disconcerting to you to see this crystallisation of the sort of criticisms you have heard. It might be helpful to remember that this same public will have forgotten it all by tomorrow.'

'Thank you, Miss Blanchard,' the Head said, smiling at last. Soon everyone was talking at once and the heavy atmosphere of gloomy concern was breaking up.

'Sir, what about the Christmas parties?' someone asked. Already other things were claiming our attention.

On December 6th, Seales was not in his place and I marked him absent. Just before recess he came in and walked briskly to my table.

'Sorry I can't stay. Sir, but my mother died early this morning and I'm helping my dad with things.'

As if those words finally broke all his efforts to be strong and grown up, his face crumpled and he wept like the small boy he really felt. I got up quickly and led him unresisting to my chair, where he sat, his head in his hands, sobbing bitterly.

I gave the news to the class: they received it in shocked silence, in that immediate sympathy and compassion which only the young seem to know and experience, and then many of them were weeping too.

I spoke comfortingly to Seales and sent him home; then I went to see Mr Florian to acquaint him with the circumstances.

After recess, as I was about to begin our History lesson, Barbara Pegg stood up; she had been asked by the class to say that they had agreed to make a collection among themselves to purchase a wreath or other floral token of sympathy, to be sent to Seales' home. I said I was agreeable, providing I was allowed to contribute also. We learned that the funeral was fixed for the Saturday. Barbara collected contributions throughout the week, and by Friday morning had nearly two pounds. I was delighted at this news, and after assembly we discussed together the type of floral token they wished to purchase and the nearest florist from whom it could be obtained. Then I remarked:

'Which of you will take it over to his home?'

Their reaction was like a cold douche. The pleasantly united cameraderie disappeared completely from the room, and in its place was the watchful antagonism I had encountered on my first day. It was as if I had pulled a thick transparent screen between them and myself, effectively shutting us away from each other.

It was ugly to see; I felt excluded, even hated, but all so horribly quickly.

'What's the matter with you?' My voice was loud in my ears, 'What's suddenly so awful about the flowers?'

Moira stood up, 'We can't take them, Sir.'

'What do you mean, Miss Joseph? Why can't you take them?'

She looked quickly around the room as if pleading with the others to help her explain.

'It's what people would say if they saw us going to a coloured person's home.' She sat down.

There it was. I felt weak and useless, an alien among them, All the weeks and months of delightful association were washed out by those few words.

Nothing had really mattered, the teaching, the talking, the example, the patience, the worry. It was all as nothing. They, like the strangers on buses and trains, saw only the skins, never the people in those skins. Scales was born among them, grew up among them, played with them; his mother was white, British, of their stock and background and beginnings.

All the hackneyed clichés hammered in my head. A coloured boy with a white mother, a West Indian boy with an English mother. Always the same. Never an English boy with a Negro or West Indian father. No, that would be placing the emphasis on his Englishness, his identification with them.

It was like a disease, and these children whom I loved without caring about *their* skins or *their* backgrounds, they were tainted with the hateful virus which attacked their vision, distorting everything that was not white or English.

I remembered a remark of Weston's: 'They're morons, cold as stone, nothing matters to them, nothing.'

I turned and walked out of the classroom, sick at heart. I wanted to talk to someone about it, but to whom? They were all white, all of them, even Gillian, so what could they say that was different. Maybe they were, by education and breeding, better able to hide it, to gloss it over with fine words.

I walked into the Head's office. He listened, his face mirroring the deep humanity and sympathy which were so truly a part of him.

'I'm glad this has happened, Braithwaite, for your sake, especially.'

'Why, Sir?'

'Because I think you were setting too much store by quick results. After all, we are not concerned here merely with academic effort; our idea is to teach them to live with one another, sharing, caring, helping. It's not easy for them.'

Here we go again, I thought. Everything those little bastards do is right, even this. Was he never prepared to see any point of view except that which supported their case?

'Whether it is easy or not, Mr Florian, Seales is one of them, he has grown up with them, he's no stranger like myself.'

'This is a community with many strong racial and religious tensions and prejudices, most of them of long standing.'

'That may be so, Sir, but Mrs Seales was a white woman of this area, and she worked at the local laundry with many other parents of these children; they knew her as well as they know her son.'

I was feeling angry with him for his attempt to excuse their conduct.

'You have been taking too much for granted, because of your success in the classroom. I am sure that they all like Seales very much, but once outside the school things are different, and I think Seales would be the first to appreciate that.'

'But Mr Florian. . . .'

'You must be patient, Mr Braithwaite,' he continued, rising. 'You've been here, how long? From May to now, nearly seven months, and you've done a great deal with them. Be patient. Maybe next year, the year after – who knows? Go back to them and show them some of the same tolerance and patient goodwill you hope to get from them.'

The little man always seemed to grow larger as he spoke; as if to compensate for his twisted frame he had been given a saintliness, a deep patient wisdom which quite dwarfed bigger, more imposing men.

After leaving the Headmaster I stood for a time in the corridor outside my classroom, my mind in a whirl. The way these children and their parents felt about Seales and his parents was a personal lesson to me. This was the sort of ostracism Gillian and I would have to face and the thought of it filled me with worry. What, I wondered, would it do to her? Would we be able to cope with it? Or would we escape it, at least in its cruder form, if we lived in different surroundings, among people who could claim better social and educational advantages? I went in.

They were quiet in the classroom. I wanted to say something, but no words came. Jacqueline Bender rose.

'Sir, I don't think you understood just now. We have nothing against Seales. We like him, honest we do, but if one of us girls was seen going to his home, you can't imagine the things people would say. We'd be accused of all sorts of things.' She sat, evidently overcome by this long speech.

'Thank you for making that so clear, Miss Bender. Does the same thing apply to the boys as well?'

They were not defiant now, but their eyes were averted.

'I'll take them.' Pamela stood up, tall and proudly regal.

'Why should you, Miss Dare? Aren't you afraid of what might be said of you?'

'No, Sir, gossips don't worry me. After all, I've known Larry, I mean Seales, since in the Infants.'

'Thank you, Miss Dare. The funeral is at ten o'clock. I'll take my usual train and perhaps I'll see you there. Thank you.'

I left it at that, pleased and encouraged by her words, and we returned to our lessons.

That evening I told Gillian of the boy's mother's death but made no mention of the other thing. I wanted to try and forget it as quickly as possible.

On Saturday morning I caught an early bus from Brentwood. I sat on the top deck in the rearmost seat, disinclined to see or be seen, to speak or be spoken to; withdrawn and wishing only to be as far removed from white people as I possibly could be. I had given all I could to those children, even part of myself, but it had been of no use. In the final analysis they had trotted out the same hoary excuse so familiar to their fathers and grandfathers: 'We have nothing against him personally, but. . . .' How well I knew it now! If he'd been pimp or pansy, moron or murderer, it would not have mattered, providing he was white; his outstanding gentleness, courtesy and intelligence could not offset the greatest sin of all, the sin of being black.

They had been glib at the Students' Council, and bright and persuasive. It had sounded great coming from them, that talk of common heritage and inalienable rights; glib and easy, until they were required to do something to back up all the talk, and then the façade had cracked and crumbled because it was as phoney as themselves. Crucify him because he's black; lynch him because he's black; ostracise him because he's black; a little change, a little shift in geographical position and they'd be using the very words they'd now so vociferously condemned.

The whir and rattle of the bus was a rhythmic percussion syncopating the anger in my heart into a steady, throbbing hate, until I felt rather light-headed. I disembarked outside the London Hospital and walked towards Commercial Road and Priddle Street where the Seales lived. As I turned into the narrow roadway I could see the drearily ornate hearse parked there, and the small group of curiosity-seekers who somehow always materialise to gape open-mouthed on the misery of others. And then I stopped, feeling suddenly washed clean, whole and alive again. Tears were in my eyes, unashamedly, for there, standing in a close, separate group on the pavement outside Seales' door was my class, my children, all or nearly all of them, smart and self-conscious in their best clothes. O God, forgive me for the hateful thoughts, because I love them, these brutal, disarming bastards, I love them . . .

I hurried over to join them to be again with them, a part of them. They welcomed me silently, pride and something else shining in their eyes as they gathered close around me. I felt something soft pressed into my hand, and as I looked round into the clear, shining eyes of Pamela Dare, I dried my own eyes with the tiny handkerchief.

CHAPTER 21

THESE LAST DAYS of term were for me the happiest I had known since leaving the R.A.F. My life was full of my work and Gillian. We grew closer together each day, our interests and delights broadened and enhanced by being shared. I met her parents as arranged. They were evidently both very nice people faced with an unexpected and difficult situation, and doing their best to be as 'civilised' as possible about it. They had reared their daughter to be independent in thought and behaviour, and made no attempt now to influence her. Besides, they loved her deeply and were primarily concerned for her happiness. I suppose I was rather on the defensive with them, watchful for any sign of enmity or patronage. They too were somewhat ill-at-ease.

Supporters of racial prejudice are fond of posing the query: 'Would you allow your daughter to marry a Negro?' I have spoken to many English parents who, feeling safe against such a contingency, have unhesitatingly asserted their willingness to allow their offspring to marry whom they choose, and the very glibness of their assertions has caused me to doubt. Now I was placing these people in a position where they must both ask themselves and answer the question. They were well established and reasonably prosperous, with the associations and responsibilities attendant upon their social position; theirs was no easy decision, and in my heart I was very sympathetic.

Before meeting Gillian I had not thought of marrying a white woman, nor had I wished to. I had met them socially and even knew a few very intimately, but had never entertained the least thought of marrying them. Not because I had anything against any of them; they were very nice, intelligent, companionable people; but because of the deep prejudice I knew existed against mixed marriages. Then out of the blue I met Gillian, and all my carefully reasoned arguments faded like mist before the sun. From the very first she fitted so easily, so completely into my life that I would not have cared if she had been blue or green. We both believed we were complementary one to the other and would strenuously have resisted any interference from anyone. We both agreed that her parents, like my own, deserved the courtesy of full information. So, here I was, willingly submitting to their scrutiny though alert for any sign of interference.

We lunched together and chatted about inconsequential places and things. They asked about myself and my parents, my education and war service, of my plans for the future and the possibilities of fulfilling them. I believe they were satisfied with my answers, yet something was missing, some necessary catalyst to bring us together into closer harmony.

Later, while we were all having a cigarette in the lounge before a cheerful fire, Mr Blanchard began to speak about South America. Before the war he had, in the course of his business, visited some of the republics and even some of the off-shore islands. He mentioned Aruba.

I knew Aruba quite well, for after graduating from University I had worked there for a short while as a technologist for the Standard Oil Company in the San Nicholas Refinery, and soon we were involved in a pleasant discussion about the island, its people, and its economic importance in the world of oil, due very largely to the large natural harbour at San Nicholas and its nearness to the huge oilfields of mainland Maracaibo.

'What's that odd language the natives use?' he asked.

'Papiamento. It's a patois composed of Dutch, Spanish and the indigent Indian dialect. Before I left it had even assumed a rather strong American flavour.'

'Do you speak it?' Mrs Blanchard wanted to know.

'Tolerably well. With a knowledge of Spanish the rest comes easily.'

'I remember seeing some of the natives in Oranjestad, riding those little donkeys of theirs,' continued Mr Blanchard.

'Burros.'

'Yes, burros.'

'Quiet, dignified people, those Arubans.'

Small talk, anything to keep us away from discussing Gillian and me.

'That's a fine club they built at Lago Heights,' I said.

'Yes, I played a lot of basketball there, and volleyball.'

'That's a real man's game.'

'It's a man's town. Men everywhere and more men.' Suddenly he laughed, amused, remembering. '*Hija del Dia*,' he said.

I stared at him and breathed a short prayer of thanks for my dark skin that hid the blushes warming my face.

'Don't you remember it?' he pursued.

His wife and Gillian exchanged glances. I stammered, 'Oh, yes,' trying with my eyes to signal him off the subject.

'Oh, don't worry, I've told them about it.'

Good grief, these English people were full of surprises! How did one describe such subjects to nice people?

'Did you ever see inside?' He was amused at my embarrassment.

'Not me, I gave it a wide berth.'

'God, those queues!' He was rocking with laughter, remembering; at ease now, forgetting to weigh, to assess, to scrutinise. This was the catalyst we had needed – these shared memories of Aruba and the Club and the queues.

They were the longest queues I have ever seen and the most memorable. Queues of men, old men and young men, white men and dark men, men in clean crisp linen and men soiled from work on a long eight-hour shift, chatting or silent, but all patiently waiting their turn to get into the big, bright painted building to pay the high prices demanded for the island's most rationed commodity, Women.

To someone like myself, fresh from the comfort and plenty

of normal American life, Aruba's hardships were exciting and easily to be borne, for they were mainly of short duration. Up-to-date American planning provided well-stocked stores where fruit, vegetables, meat and other perishables could be obtained, fresh and crisp out of huge refrigerators. Nothing grew on the island except cactus, and these were gigantic, with thorns four to five inches long, as if Nature were indulging in one of her occasional jokes by encouraging these useless things when even grass successfully resisted the most devoted attention. Even fresh water was brought to the island by tanker fleet to supplement the output of the ageing plant which converted seawater into a flat, brackish all-purpose liquid.

But the real shortage was Women. The refinery was built, managed, and developed by Americans and provided employment for tens of thousands of white and coloured men from the U.S.A., the Caribbean Islands and the South American mainland, together with many able-bodied indigenous Arubans. All day and all night these thousands were on the move to and from the refinery gates in an unending three-shift cycle; they crowded the shops, restaurants, bodegas and cafés.

But the sight of a woman was rare, for there was then no prepared accommodation for the wives of the men who flocked to the well-paid jobs from as far south as Montevideo, and who were housed cheek by jowl in hastily fabricated ranges of tiny cubicles, sharing communal dining halls and toilet facilities. A far-sighted and practical Aruban Government permitted (possibly even designed) a certain degree of easement to the situation. Prostitutes, some of them very young and innocent looking, were allowed to visit the island from the various mainland seaports and inland towns, on a two-week return ticket, and to ply their trade under somewhat close medical supervision. The women arrived by the twice-monthly inter-island steamer, which soon became known as 'The Meat Boat'. Most of them were housed in the big, garish building not far from the refinery's main gates, with its huge sign *Hija del Dia*, 'Daughter of the Day', and soon after the word went around, 'The meat boat's in,' the queues of men would begin to form outside its doors, jocularly speeding the tired departees, and eagerly welcoming the replacements.

I looked at Mr Blanchard, trying to picture him there. As if divining my thoughts he smiled, and said:

'I never went in either. I was there for two days doing some business for the British-Dutch Shell people at Oranjestad; a friend drove me out to the Lago Club for drinks and I saw them. God, what a life! I'll never forget those queues.'

On Sunday afternoon after lunch we all sat down to discuss the matter which was uppermost in all our minds. Gillian's parents were very frank in expressing their opinion. Mr Blanchard said:

'I'm going to hand it to you straight, Ricky. When we first heard that Gillian was seeing you, her mother and I talked about it, but we decided not to interfere, hoping that it was just one of those things and would blow over.

'When Gillian wrote that she was bringing you down here, we realised that it was more serious than we had imagined. We know our daughter, Rick, and we felt sure that this must be important to her; after meeting you it is not difficult to understand why.' He got up and lit his pipe, then sat on the arm of Gillian's chair. 'We would, even now, prefer that Gillian had fallen in love with someone of her own colour; it would have made everything so much easier for her as well as for us. Before this I would have unhesitatingly asserted that I was without prejudice, racial or otherwise, but now that it has reached me to become a personal, intimate issue, I know that I would do anything in my power to break this up, if I thought it would do any good. It's not just the two of you, Rick, that have to be considered. You might have children; what happens to them? They'll belong nowhere, and nobody will want them.'

I had listened to him patiently and respectfully, because he was an older man and even more because he was Gillian's father. But there he was, so big and sure of himself, mouthing the same old excuses, the same old arguments, hitting below the belt. I had heard it all before.

'I don't think the children would be anyone's business but our own, Mr Blanchard,' I retorted, as calmly as I could. 'If Gillian and I marry, I hope we have children and those children will belong to us and we will want them.'

I looked at Gillian, wishing her with me in this, hoping I was truly speaking for both of us; she smiled at me, with her eyes and her lips and her heart, encouraging me.

'You need not worry about us, Sir, or about our children. I don't suppose you were able to offer Mrs Blanchard any guarantees that her children would be strong, healthy or without physical deformity. We, too, will take our chance, though I appreciate how very inconvenient it might be for you to have coloured grandchildren.'

He blushed at this remark, but was determined to be as civilised as possible, and raised his hand to silence any further retort.

'No need to become too heated, young man, you have made your point. Don't forget that Gillian is our daughter, and marrying you will not change that.'

I sat down and waited for him to continue.

'I'm saying these things to you quite dispassionately, as her father; other people will think and say them, probably in very unpleasant terms. I want you two young people to understand thoroughly the very difficult step you are taking.' He suddenly smiled at me and went on: 'We like you, Rick, and hope this works out for both of your sakes. But we think it would be wise if you waited a while, say about six months at least, before taking any further action; that should give you time to get accustomed to being together and meeting people together.

'And remember,' he said, rising, 'if you're joining this family we might as well be friends.' With that he extended his hand and I shook it.

'Thank you, Sir,' I said.

CHAPTER 22

SHORTLY AFTER MY meeting with Gillian's parents the class had a visit from the district Youth Employment Officer, who spoke to them of the opportunities open to them in the local industries, mainly clothing and furniture factories, which generally absorbed the majority of those leaving school. To a great extent his efforts at recruitment had been anticipated by mothers and fathers, sisters and brothers, aunts and uncles who, already employed in those industries, were desirous of having their children with the same firm.

Some of the class sought and obtained employment farther afield, as juniors in offices. Seales was accepted for apprenticeship training with a large electrical engineering firm in Middlesex; Fernman landed a job as messenger at Cable and Wireless Ltd; Tich Jackson was promised a job as page in a big London hotel; Potter was accepted in some capacity at Covent Garden market; Denham had made up his mind to be his own boss and his father agreed to set him up in business as a barrow-boy. Pamela and Barbara were to be trainees with a West End firm of bespoke dressmakers, and Pamela's mother felt sure that her girl could eventually be taught modelling because of her fine figure and upright, easy carriage. They were all dispersing like feathers to the four winds.

At first they had spoken eagerly and impatiently of leaving school, earning money, buying clothes, going places; but now, as their remaining days dwindled away, they became subdued, even frightened at the prospect of fixed hours and supervised work. But not afraid of life. They were hesitant

176

about taking the first step, the initial plunge into the stream, but they were not afraid of the stream itself. They felt sure that they had learned to swim; they were strong, fearless and full of cheerful enthusiasm, all of which would help them to keep afloat. They might need to adapt their strokes, control their breathing, or alter course in the face of currents or obstructions, but they were not afraid.

I got to know them even better than before; they were in a hurry to say all that was to be said while there was still time, and during the last week there was not a single absence.

One girl even asked to be allowed to bring her baby sister to school with her, while the mother attended hospital for dental treatment. The baby lay peacefully in her carry-cot, her gurgling a pleasant diversion in the classroom.

We talked. No formal lessons were possible in this atmosphere of excitement, so we talked, especially about the relationship between peoples. I listened to their views and was surprised and delighted at some of the things they said.

They had been reared in a neighbourhood as multi-racial as anywhere in Britain, yet it had been of no significance to them. Some of them lived in the same street, the same block of flats, as Indians or Negroes, without ever even speaking to them, in obedience to the parental taboo. Others had known and grown up with coloured children through the Infant and Junior stages, but when the tensions and pretensions of puberty had intervened the relationship had ended.

They wanted me to tell them what they ought to do to help in the achievement of better inter-racial unity in their own neighbourhood. I reminded them of the History and Geography we had read, of people, places and things. I tried to show them that people were not confined to any geographical location because of their colour, but that there could be found people of every racial strain in all parts of the world. Once there, wherever it was, they could get along with each other if they really wanted to.

It is not necessary for them to do anything special for a Negro or Indian, or any other person, but simply to behave to them as to a stranger Briton, without favour or malevolence, but with the courtesy and gentleness which every human being should give to and expect from every other.

I made it clear that it was also true that coloured people in England were gradually working for their own salvation, realising that it was not enough for them to complain about injustices done them, or rely on other interested parties to agitate on their behalf. They were working to show their worth, integrity and dignity in spite of the forces opposed to them.

On Wednesday morning during recess Clinty breezed into my classroom, smiling as archly as the cat who ate the canary. 'How goes, Rick?' she greeted me.

I wondered what was up and murmured some greeting in reply; what on earth was cooking in that pretty Cockney head?

'I just heard that Miss Blanchard might be leaving at the end of next term,' she announced quite gaily. I looked up, startled by this information; Gillian had said nothing to me about leaving. 'Oh, when did you hear that?' I tried to keep the surprise out of my voice.

'The Old Man was making the usual check-up for next term's staffing, and it seems that she told him she would be here next term but could not commit herself to any time after that.' She perched herself in her favourite place on the edge of my desk.

'Did she give any special reason?' I wanted to play this along, taking my lead from anything Gillian might have said; we had agreed to keep our business as much as possible to ourselves, away from staffroom gossip.

'Just got fed up with slumming, I suppose,' she chirped. I smiled in relief. Good old Gillian.

'You don't like her, do you, Clinty?'

'Oh, I don't mind her at all, but I've met her superior type before. I can't say I would exactly miss her.' She was really quite pleased with herself.

'I find her a very charming, intelligent person, Clinty.'

'So I've noticed,' she countered. 'Well, when she's gone I suppose you'll have to be content with the rest of us ordinary types.'

'Don't fish, Clinty. You're all nice people here, or nearly all.'

She smiled at that and I switched the subject. 'By the way, what's the gen on arrangements for tomorrow?'

'Big do,' she replied, 'Christmas dinner in the dining hall. The Old Man likes everybody to be there, so you'll have to miss your little lunch tête-à-tête, I'm afraid.'

I laughed at this; if only she knew. We talked on about the programme for the next two days and she left as the bell rang. She had come about something else I felt sure, but it didn't come out. Maybe just as well.

Thursday morning I saw very little of my class. The girls were in the Domestic Science Department preparing the spread for the Christmas party that afternoon; the boys were pressed into service by Grace, and were busy cleaning pots and pans, and generally helping with the heavier chores. I peeped in there for a while and was very pleased to see them all working in an atmosphere of lively co-operation. They trooped down to the classroom about twelve-twenty and crowded around me, chattering gaily, until the bell rang for dinner.

The dining hall looked festive with paper chains and balloons strung from the windows, and along the walls. The kitchen staff had prepared an excellent meal – roast pork, baked potatoes and all the trimmings; for dessert there was trifle, which the children loved. After the Head had said a short prayer, he made a signal and from the door at the far end of the hall two small girls entered, bearing between them a large cellophane-wrapped bouquet of flowers. Down the long aisle they walked, through the question-laden quiet, towards Mrs Drew; they handed her the bouquet, dropped two very pretty curtsies and quickly hurried away to their places.

Mrs Drew blushed deeply. I rather suspected that it had been carefully planned by the Head as a token of the high regard in which this gracious person was held. Someone shouted 'Speech, speech' and soon there was a general clamour. She rose with that graceful dignity which never deserted her and seemed prepared to address them, but, as if her courage had suddenly failed, she merely said, 'Thank you,' and sat down to a burst of cheering.

The junior party was at three o'clock, in the auditorium. I did not enjoy it. The room, like the dining hall, had been festooned with paper chains and balloons and looked very gay, but it was all spoilt for me by the behaviour of most of the smaller children. They wolfed the food down greedily, snatching at anything which caught their fancy, shouting across at each other. The seniors were busy serving them and were somewhat disgruntled at their rudeness and bad manners; I was thoroughly disgusted, especially with those who would bite into a bit of cake or pastry and then discard it for something else. Mr Florian seemed quite unperturbed by the noisy, unpleasant exhibition, but moved easily among them helping here and there, as if he rather expected such conduct. I was quite relieved when the last morsels had disappeared and the children were dismissed.

We all helped to clear up the mess, and mess it really was. The big boys brought brooms, mops and pails from the kitchen, and soon the tables were cleared away, and the floor was tidy and shining once more. They were happy to do it, because at six o'clock the senior party would begin. A few tables were set together in one corner of the room and on these were piled the buffet of refreshments; the record-player was ready and there was a pile of dance records which would be supplemented by personal choice from the children's own collections. Some of the Old Boys and Old Girls had been invited and we expected quite a gathering. At about four o'clock the seniors went home to pretty themselves up. Pamela met me in the corridor. 'Please, Sir,' she said, 'will you have a dance with me tonight?'

'Of course, Miss Dare,' I replied, 'but not jiving – I'm getting too old for that sort of thing.'

. She laughed gaily at that. 'Okay, Sir, I'll bring a special record for you. Promise?'

'Yes, Miss Dare, I promise.'

'And Sir.'

'Yes?'

'Will you call me Pamela, just for this evening?'

'Of course, Pamela . . .'

All the staff were on hand to meet the children when they arrived. Denham and Potter were the earliest, looking freshly groomed and smart in their best suits and brightly polished shoes; then came Tich Jackson with his brother, a tall good-looking youth who had left Greenslade the year before and was now 'going steady' with Janie Lithgow's sister; then a small group of boys, Seales, Fernman, Buckley, Sapiano and Wells, smiling self-consciously and remaining together. The approach of the girls was heralded by much chatter and giggling on the stairs, then they burst in upon us, fresh, clean and gay as wild flowers in a mountain valley. They had been planning and saving for this occasion, and the results were very gratifying. With their lipstick and high heels they were as attractive a bunch of youngsters as anyone could hope to find anywhere.

Moira Joseph wore a plain, form-fitting black dress with long, tight, wrist-length sleeves, unrelieved by ornament of any kind. With her close-cropped hair, thick eyebrows and very bright lipstick, she looked like a sophisticated young woman, slim, elegant and poised. Barbara Pegg's tight lacy blouse and dirndl skirt were freshly, appealingly youthful and set off her freckles delightfully.

But the belle of the ball was Pamela, a new, beautiful, grown-up Pamela. Her hair was caught high on the back of her head but slightly to one side with a glistening ribbon of dark green silk, from which it fell away in a cascade of soft tendrilly curls to her right shoulder. Her full lips were vividly red against the clear face and the long, lovely neck. She wore a simple dress of dark green jersey wool, softly clinging at shoulder, bosom and waist, and flaring to a wide skirt which did wonderful things for her as she walked. Her shoes were of green satin. She presented a picture of sheer beauty and I gazed at her in wonder, seeing quite clearly her mother's skilful hand in its preparation.

'Good Lord,' Gillian exclaimed as Pamela walked into the

Auditorium, 'that girl's beautiful!' There was something very like awe in her voice. Pamela walked across to us. 'Hello, Sir. Hello, Miss,' she greeted us.

'Hello, Pamela,' we echoed.

'You haven't forgotten, have you, Sir?' Pamela enquired, her eyes on me.

'No, I haven't forgotten, Pamela,' I replied.

'See you, Sir,' and she moved over to join some of her colleagues.

'She never even saw me,' Gillian whispered.

'Oh course she did, she said "Hello" to both of us,' I reminded her.

'Oh I know, but she didn't really see me, she just didn't see me.' Her voice was quietly intense, and I turned to look at her, wondering at her tone. She looked up at me and grinned, then reached for my hand.

'Thank Heaven I got to you first, Rick,' she whispered, seeming not to care who noticed us now.

Soon the room was nearly full of laughing, joyous young people. I was introduced to several of the Old Students who had been invited. Jackie Fischer, Junie Thorpe, Ada Phillips, Petey Blore and Maureen Blore the twins, whose sister Ann introduced us. Maureen invited me to attend the reception of her wedding on Boxing Day.

It was a very happy occasion. We danced and played silly enjoyable games, the staff all as joyously boisterous as the youngsters. Even Weston so far forgot himself as to laugh and chatter quite naturally with them. He could not dance but elected to be responsible for the music, and he seemed to enjoy being Master of Ceremonies, announcing each record before it began. Later in the evening he offered me a cigarette and we exchanged a few pleasantries. The spirit of goodwill was in operation with a vengeance; I hoped it would survive well into the next term.

Whenever I could I danced with Gillian. Just being near her was peace and pleasure beyond words; I felt sure that our love for each other must be quite apparent to anyone with eyes to see. Later, while I was dancing a Strauss waltz with Clinty, she said:

'You're really gone on her, aren't you Rick?'

'Who?'

'Ah, come off it. I'm talking about Miss Blanchard.'

Neither Clinty nor any of the others ever called her anything but Miss Blanchard; something about her seemed to prohibit too-easy intimacy.

'Well, what about her?'

'Okay, Rick. I can take a hint, but if it is what I think it is between you two, you're a damned lucky tyke.'

I laughed, just for the hell of it.

Soon after, Pamela went up to Weston with her record; they whispered together, then he announced:

'The next dance is a "Ladies' Excuse-me Foxtrot".'

She waited until the first few opening bars of the beautiful evergreen 'In the Still of the Night' floated over the room then turned and walked towards me, invitation large in her clear eyes and secretly smiling lips. I moved to meet her and she walked into my arms, easily, confidently, as if she belonged there. There was no hesitation, no pause to synchronise our steps; the music and the magic of the moment took us and wove us together in smooth movement. I was aware of her, of her soft breathing, her firm roundness, and the rhythmic moving of her thighs. She was a woman, there was no doubt about it, and she invaded my mind and my body. The music ended, all too soon. We were locked together for a moment, then released.

'Thank you, Pamela.'

'After I leave school may I come and see you sometimes?'

'Of course, I'd be very pleased to see you any time.'

'Thank you. 'Bye, Sir.'

''Bye, Pamela.'

She collected her record from Weston and left soon afterwards.

Next morning, Friday, they were very quiet. As I called the register, going through the list of now familiar names I thought of how very quickly the time had passed since the first day I had sat there, uncertain and a little afraid. In about eight months I had come to know them all so well: now I could nearly anticipate the things they would say and do in any given circumstance. Yet after today most of them would be going their different ways and as remote from me as if we had never met.

Some of them had grown strong from within – Fernman, Babs Pegg, Wells, Seales, these would make the grade because they were intelligent, resourceful, and ever willing to learn. Some would always have difficulties, because they wanted the easy way out, quick money with the least possible effort, Sapiano and Janie Purcell, for instance. But the rest of them would just be decent folk, living decently without too much ambition or aggressiveness or anything. Denham and Potter. In a few years they'd both be dependable, hard-working men with families, or maybe serving somewhere overseas in H.M. Forces. Who could know?

Registration over, they began talking excitedly about the evening before, the clothes, the food, the records, the dancing, the staff – everything. They had enjoyed it, particularly the company of adults whom they had met on equal terms; it had been important, 'posh', different from the usual 'hops' at the local youth clubs. I came in for a bit of ribbing because they had noticed how often I danced with Gillian.

'Is she your girl, Sir?' Tich Jackson enquired.

'I noticed you dancing with Miss Blanchard too, Jackson.' I parried, 'I was beginning to wonder if she was your girl.'

'Gosh, wouldn't mind if she was,' Jackson replied, to a burst of laughter from the others. And so the morning passed, in a sluggish friendliness, a disinclination to let the moments go.

In the afternoon after registration I sat looking at them, uncertain what to say to them. Just then Moira Joseph stood up.

'Sir,' she began, 'I, that is, we want to tell you how very grateful we are for all you have done for us, all of us.' She looked slowly round the room. 'We know it could not have been too easy for you, what with one thing or another,' here she smiled at Denham, who blushed and hung his head, 'but you kept going. We think we are much better children for having had you as a teacher. We liked best the way you always talked to us, you know, not like silly kids, but like grown-ups and that. You've been good to us, Sir, and we'd like you to accept a little gift to remember us by.' Here she signalled to Pamela and sat down amid a burst of cheering.

Pamela stood up, with a large beautifully wrapped parcel in her hand, and walked towards me. I rose at her approach. She was a striking figure as she came proudly up with the parcel, but no sooner had I received it from her hand than she suddenly turned and ran back to her seat to hide her face behind the lid of her desk. At a moment when she so wanted to be at her grown-up best, childhood had claimed her again.

I thanked them and sat down quickly, as the door opened and Mr Florian walked quietly in: he had been attracted by the noise of cheering. Together we looked at the large label pasted on the parcel and inscribed:

TO SIR,
WITH LOVE

and underneath, the signatures of all of them.

He looked at me and smiled. And I looked over his shoulder at them – my children.

THE HISTORY OF VINTAGE

The famous American publisher Alfred A. Knopf (1892–1984) founded Vintage Books in the United States in 1954 as a paperback home for the authors published by his company. Vintage was launched in the United Kingdom in 1990 and works independently from the American imprint although both are part of the international publishing group, Random House.

Vintage in the United Kingdom was initially created to publish paperback editions of books bought by the prestigious literary hardback imprints in the Random House Group such as Jonathan Cape, Chatto & Windus, Hutchinson and later William Heinemann, Secker & Warburg and The Harvill Press. There are many Booker and Nobel Prize-winning authors on the Vintage list and the imprint publishes a huge variety of fiction and non-fiction. Over the years Vintage has expanded and the list now includes great authors of the past – who are published under the Vintage Classics imprint – as well as many of the most influential authors of the present. In 2012 Vintage Children's Classics was launched to include the much-loved authors of our youth.

For a full list of the books Vintage publishes,
please visit our website
www.vintage-books.co.uk

For book details and other information about the classic authors we publish, please visit the Vintage Classics website
www.vintage-classics.info